The River Rats

Bethany,
Books can take
you anywhere.
Read! Read! Read!

The River Rats

Hank Racer

Enjoy the adventure,
Hank Racer

To John
The best little brother ever.

To Jan
Who would never let me give up or give in.

To all the River Rats – Past, Present and Future

To Adrian Fogelin
Who gave me the inspiration to write what I
already knew.

A special thanks to my editor – Emily Carmain

Thanks also to:
Family, friends and colleagues for their enthusiastic
support and especially to Elizabeth Racer Hooks,
Christopher Hooks, Hugh and Frances Keiser,
Darlene Eaton, Connie Conner and the students at
Swimming Pen Creek Elementary, Kathleen Choate,
Bill Reynolds and Jennifer Wehrmann.

The River Rat group:

Erick Pitman –**"Moe"** – Had looked like Moe from the Three Stooges when he was born.

Jessie Mathas – **"Tank"** – Had always been big. Weighed over ten pounds when born. Doctor gave him his nickname.

Alton James Warton DeLagere – **"Wart"** – Small of stature and named Warton.

Harold Simmons – **"Dill"** – Loves dill pickles.

Bobby Toothman Simmons – **"Tooth"** – Refers to middle name and an unnatural looking tooth.

Everett Eugene Pitman – **"Eep"** – Erick's little brother. Initials are EEP.

General Stonewall Jackson – **"The General"** – Eep's dog of unknown origin.

Prologue

❧—The Ohio River begins in Pittsburgh, Pennsylvania, and flows south to where it creates the border between the states of Ohio and West Virginia. Commercial boats travel up and down the river hauling everything from aluminum ore from South America for the giant aluminum processing mills, to coal on its way to power plants across the United States and around the world.

The river at times drags all sorts of things along with it on its way to the Mississippi River. Sometimes it will grab a house when it floods. Other times it will take a tree whose roots have finally given out along the river's banks. But, sometimes, it will pick up things that are unexpected, like a body.

railroad tracks below. There might have been a happy ending to this tragedy except for the bridge that stood directly in the truck's path.

The metal girders of the bridge took the impact of the truck, sending it jack-knifing high into the air. As the wheels of the trailer became entwined with the crushed steel girders, the truck swung over the side of the bridge, finally coming to a halt hanging precariously over the edge of the bridge. The two men in the cab of the truck were now dangling in mid-air.

Looking out the front window, the driver could see the water of the muddy creek below. Beside him, he could see his friend who had been thrown up against the window. The bones of his friend's left arm stuck out in several places, while blood streamed down his face.

Moving towards his injured friend, the driver felt a sharp pain in his side. Only then did he spot the blood on his shirt just above his waist. With great effort he unpinned himself from behind the steering wheel. The passenger began to stir as the driver tugged on his shoulder, trying to see if he was free enough to escape.

At that moment, one of the wheels on the truck tore loose from the bridge above. The truck fell ten feet before suddenly halting its descent. The driver and his passenger again slammed against the dashboard.

The driver tried to rouse his friend, but finding him lodged against the dash, he gave up and began crawling out of the window.

Above, two men were tying ropes to the bridge in hopes that they could lower someone down to help the truck's trapped occupants.

In the early morning light, the driver's head could barely be seen as it appeared through the window. The men above hurriedly tossed one of the ropes in his direction. Missing the rope on the first toss, the driver caught it on the second. When he had securely tied it around his waist, he looked back inside the truck.

Seeing the passenger stir, he screamed, "Wade. Wade can you hear me?"

Leaning back inside the truck's cab, he made one last effort to pull his friend free. The passenger's legs came out from under the dashboard just as a loud crack came from above.

The driver crawled back out the window as the truck started slowly inching downward. Ducking his head out of the window, the driver was swept back up the side of the truck as it fell. Luckily his shoulder hit the exhaust pipe behind the driver's door pushing him out and away from the truck as it sped towards the muddy creek below.

The two men above held on to the rope until several more people joined them in their tug-of-war effort to save the driver, who was now swinging wildly fifty feet below them.

Chapter Two

•❖—Maye Vern Wheatly didn't notice the pair of red eyes that stared at her as she untied the stern mooring line of the fourteen-foot runabout she and her husband Calmus took out for a ride on the Ohio River each Wednesday afternoon in the summer. Standing barely five feet tall, she looked about as wide. Dressed in a matching orange blouse and pedal-pushers with a wide brimmed Panama straw hat, she resembled an oversized pumpkin ready for harvest.

The runabout, named Maye-I-Go, was tied up to a one-hundred-foot-long floating dock pretentiously known as the Monley Yacht Club. The dock had wooden planks attached to fifty-five-gallon oil drums that were constantly in motion, making it hard for Maye Vern to keep her balance.

Calmus, Cal to his friends, looked much like his wife, short and wide. Calmus had been hunched over facing up river, untying the boat's bow line, when his wife gave out a guttural scream that brought the hair up on the back of his neck and could be heard clear over on the Ohio side of the river.

The ghostly face broke the surface of the murky Ohio River just as Maye Vern started to stand up. The red eyes looked straight at her with a penetrating stare. Moving up and down, the mouth looked as if it was trying to talk to her. Then suddenly, through the gurgling water, came the hushed sound of, "Follow me. I'll show you the way."

Maye Vern could hardly catch her breath as she jumped to her feet. She closed her eyes, trying to break the gaze of the ghostly thing staring up at her from the muddy water. As the scream that started deep within her finally reached her mouth, she stumbled backwards on the slowly rocking dock and reached the edge without realizing it. She looked down, seeing only the murky water as she took one last step still trying to regain her balance. Her right foot sailed high into the air as her left reached down for the water. She looked like a high-stepping drum major leading a band in a parade. Unfortunately for Maye Vern, a small skiff caught her left arm as she fell backwards, wrenching her shoulder and breaking her arm as she disappeared into the dirty water.

Calmus ran to where his wife had fallen into the water, but could see no trace of her anywhere. Only her straw hat floating on the surface of the river gave a clue that something terribly wrong had just happened. The dark silent water had engulfed Maye Vern and gave no indication where she might be. Calmus' whole life revolved around his wife and the bank he ran as its president. At that moment the bank meant nothing. He felt only a huge emptiness in the pit of his stomach.

"Oh God, please. Where is she?" he screamed.

As his scream ended, Maye Vern's head popped up out of the water sputtering and coughing. Immediately Calmus jumped into the dark water and paddled towards his wife.

Her right arm beat the water furiously as she tried to stay afloat. Her left arm hung useless and limp in the water. Choking and trying to scream, her eyes ablaze with fear, she grabbed for Calmus as he finally reached her.

Chapter Three

•❧—River rats are large ugly creatures with sharp teeth and long pencil-thin tails. They are a special breed of rodent that lives only along rivers or large creeks. These rats can grow to be the size of a large cat. In fact, cats run from them. Only the meanest dog will mess with them and most people are afraid of them. When backed into a corner, they will hunch their backs up and fight anything that threatens them. They are afraid of nothing. These creatures inhabit the railroad and highway tunnels that carry the small mountain streams down to the Ohio River. These animals also love to burrow up under the houses built along the river's banks.

The name River Rats is also the name taken by a group of boys who inhabited the banks of the Ohio River at Monley, West Virginia. They explored the tunnels that fed down to the river, swam in the murky waters of the Ohio, and played in the crawl spaces under their families' homes along the riverside. If the occasion to meet a real river rat came along, they might throw rocks at them, shoot them with their BB guns--or run if a real river rat attacked.

The group of six close friends included Erick Pitman, the group's leader, who was twelve years old. Moe, as the group knew him, acted as the River Rats spokesman, when they needed one. No election had taken place; everyone just always looked to him when they needed guidance. Though none of the boys would admit it, they all knew he was the smartest and best organizer in their midst. He also happened to be the strongest of the River Rats.

The biggest member of the River Rats was Jessie Mathas, also known as Tank. At age twelve, he already stood almost six feet tall and weighed close to two hundred pounds. With curly black hair and a disarming smile, he was big and good-looking.

The third twelve-year-old was Alton James Warton DeLagere. Wart was the oldest of the boys by a month, but also the smallest. Smaller even than the only ten-year-old in the group. The most athletic of the troupe, he could climb a tree faster and out-run any of the others, and like a real river rat, he feared nothing. Most of the time this served the group well, but on occasion, it had gotten them into trouble.

The two eleven-year-olds, Harold and Bobby Toothman Simmons, were affectionately known as Dill and Tooth. Because they were inseparable, the group called them the twins. Though they were now brothers, they had started out as cousins.

Tooth's mother and Dill's mother were sisters, but a rockslide on a foggy night had taken Tooth's parents when he was only five years old. From that time on he had lived with the Simmons family, being adopted and taking their name when he turned eight.

The two boys were almost exactly the same height, but they had little else physically in common. Tooth was muscular and dark headed. Dill was skinny and blonde. All the boys were good swimmers--they had to be, since one of the initiations for entering the group was to complete a swim across the mile-wide Ohio River. But Tooth and Dill were the two best swimmers, though Tooth was by far the better of the two.

The youngest member of the group was Everett Eugene Pitman, age ten. Because of his initials he had been known as Eep all his life. He was Moe's little brother and sometime pain in the neck. He constantly created problems for the group, but because Moe had to take him along when he left the house, the River Rats were stuck with him.

The last member of the group was General Stonewall Jackson, Eep's part Golden Lab and mostly mutt. The dog was particularly well suited for being a member of this group. Like the boys, he loved to swim in the river and explore the tunnels under the highway and railroad, and he especially loved to torment the real river rats when he had occasion to run into one. He loved to chase them and nip at them, but was smart enough to back off when they made a stand to fight. When this happened, he showed one other useful characteristic. He could run like the wind.

One particular day, the River Rats were on their way to the Monley City Park. Walking along River Boulevard, past the Monley Yacht Club, all six River Rats heard the deathly scream. Immediately they ran towards the river bank in the direction of the sound. As they ran to the river's edge, they could see Al Dristen, a local druggist, running towards the south end of the yacht club dock with a rope circling over his head like Roy Rogers. When he turned loose the rope, it sailed in the direction of two people thrashing about in the water. The lady seemed to be trying to crawl on top of the man with one arm while dragging the other arm behind her. The man reached for the rope, but the weight of the woman kept forcing him under the surface of the water.

Moe yelled, "Come on," as he ran down the embankment. The other five boys followed close behind.

Moe dove into the water with Tank and Dill right after him. Wart screamed at Eep to run for help. The Police Station was only three blocks away at the top of the hill, so he headed in that direction as fast as he could.

When Wart turned back around, he could see Tooth swimming towards the small runabout, which was now floating free and heading straight towards the ferryboat that took cars back and forth between Monley and Bryans Landing, across the river in Ohio. Wart dove into the murky water and swam towards the line that only minutes before, Calmus and Maye Vern Wheatly had been untying for a scenic afternoon getaway on the river.

Moe and Tank reached the Wheatlys at about the time Mr. Wheatly appeared to be giving up. Moe grabbed Mrs. Wheatly by the hair and began pulling her towards the shore. She tried to reach out with her good right arm to grab Moe, but she had about exhausted all the strength she had. Moe had little trouble pulling Mrs. Wheatly to shore.

Calmus held the rope tightly in his left hand as Tank reached him. Dill came up behind Mr. Wheatly, grabbed the collar of his shirt and pulled his head above water. Tank then took hold of Mr. Wheatly's right arm and, between them, Tank and Dill brought Mr. Wheatly to the shore.

Tooth swam towards the shore with the runabout's bowline in his right hand while Wart grabbed the stern line. Slowly they pulled the small powerboat ashore just as the back end of it ran into the ferry. After tying the runabout to a small tree along the bank they ran back to help the other River Rats.

Mrs. Wheatly kept screaming, "I saw a ghost and it talked to me. Where's Calmus? Where's Calmus?"

She kept saying over and over that she had seen a ghost and that it had talked to her.

When Tank and Dill reached the shore, they turned Mr. Wheatly on his stomach and began pushing down on his back, then pulling him up by his shoulders.

With a great shudder, Calmus Wheatly gave out a large cough and spit up half the Ohio River. He kept coughing, but seemed to be getting his breath in between coughs. After a couple of minutes, he began to breathe easier and crawled over to his wife.

"Maye Vern, are you okay?" he said tenderly. "I thought I'd lost you."

"Oh, Calmus, I saw a ghost and it was trying to say something. It was terrible. I saw a ghost and it was talking."

"It's okay, dear. It's okay," he said, hugging his wife. "Thank you, boys. You saved my life. You saved both of our lives. I owe you everything."

The police car pulled up just then and Eep jumped out of the back before either of the two police officers could open their doors.

"Moe, what happened? What did I miss? Did anyone drown?" Eep asked.

"Shut up. No one drowned. I don't know what happened," said Moe.

"Is everyone okay? What happened? Is there anyone else in the water?" Police Chief Todd asked.

Elmer Todd had been Monley's Police Chief for as long as any of the River Rats could remember. In fact, he had been Police Chief since before any of them had been born. "For twenty-two years I've had the privilege of serving the people of Monley," he liked to say.

Running up to where the police were standing, Al Dristen was chattering a mile a minute.

"I saw it all. Maye Vern stumbled and fell into the river and Calmus jumped in after her. I threw them a line just as the boys showed up. Between us we were able to save both of them."

"That's right. We showed up and Mr. and Mrs. Wheatly were in the water splashing around, so we jumped in and helped them," Moe added.

"The boat was about to float away, so we pulled it back before it hit the ferry. I think it's okay," Wart said, still a little out of breath.

"Okay, okay. Let's start at the beginning. What happened?" Chief Todd asked.

"Elmer, I think you should call an ambulance for my wife. I think she's broken her arm," said Calmus, cutting off any further discussion of the tragic event for the moment.

"Right you are, Calmus. Bobby, get on the radio and call for an ambulance. Also call ahead to the hospital and make sure Doc Ward is there," Chief Todd said authoritatively.

"Yes, sir. Right away," said Deputy Bobby Franks.

It could have been because of his tall, skinny appearance or the fact that he didn't wear a gun or that his initials were B.F., but behind his back everyone referred to Deputy Bobby Franks as "Barney Fife."

"The ambulance is on the way and Doc Ward is already at the hospital," Chief Todd said. "Now, Cal, can you tell me what happened?"

Maye Vern spoke before her husband had a chance. "I saw a ghost. Its face came right up out of the water. It stared straight at me and tried to say something to me. It was a ghost, Elmer, and it was trying to talk."

"I don't know what Maye Vern saw, Elmer. I

was at the other end of the boat, but whatever she saw really scared her. That scream about curdled my blood," said Calmus. "When I looked up, she had fallen in the water, so I jumped in after her. That's when the boys showed up. I don't know if either of us would have made it if they hadn't been there."

"That's right," Al Dristen added. "I saw it all and if it hadn't been for me and the boys here, I don't know if Cal and Maye Vern would have made it."

"Right you are, Al," said the Chief. "I can see that. The boys did help you out a bit."

Calmus again told what he knew of the frightening events, but after the third time hearing the story Chief Todd felt that not much more could be added. Something had scared Maye Vern Wheatly, which had set off the whole incident. But what? Maye Vern continued to babble on about a talking ghost in the river.

Even though he professed to have seen everything, Al Dristen had actually seen very little of what had happened. He hadn't done much either, but Al's involvement in what had happened continued to grow as his version of the story changed with each person who would listen to him. Al had a reputation of playing with the truth to suit his need for attention. Most people just passed off most of his stories, but this time people seemed to hang on his every word as he told his version of the story.

As the driver loaded Maye Vern into the ambulance, Chief Todd saw that a crowd had gathered around the entrance to the Monley Yacht Club. Some were even taking pictures.

"All right, you people, there's nothing to see here," Chief Todd said. "You people need to move along. Go on about your business."

Al Dristen had already found a couple of ears to bend and began telling his version of what had

Chapter Four

♣ As the police car started off down the street, Tooth said to no one in particular, "I saw a body."

Five heads turned immediately, looking at him.

"What?" asked Tank.

"I saw a body, or at least I think I did."

"What do you mean, you think you did? Either you saw a body or you didn't," said Dill.

"No. I mean yes. I mean..."

"What the heck do you mean?" asked Moe. "Did you see a body or didn't you? What's the deal?"

"When I swam out to get the boat line, something heavy bumped into me. I got scared at first, but then it was gone," said Tooth. "When we reached shore, I looked back and saw what looked like someone's back. It looked like a shirt with a rope for a belt around it. At least that's what I think I saw."

"Hey, you're right," Wart said. "I saw something in the water. I only caught a glimpse of it. I thought it might be a log or something, but I did see something."

"Why didn't you tell Chief Todd?" asked Moe.

"Because I'm not sure of what I saw. It wasn't until after Mrs. Wheatly started talking about a ghost that I thought maybe what I saw was a body. Then I thought they might think I was as crazy as her," said Tooth.

"Where was the body when you saw it?" "Just over there. Past where the Wheatlys' boat is tied up."

"Hey, if we can find it there might be a reward," said Eep.

"Shut up, you little twerp," said Tooth.

"You shut up," said Eep.

"I'll kick your--"

"Shut up, both of you, or I'll kick both of your butts," said Moe. "They don't give rewards for bodies, but it might be neat if we could find it."

"Well, come on. Maybe we can find it before it gets too far," said Dill.

With that, all six boys rushed down along the bank of the river and started walking south with the current. The ferryboat, Big Moses, had already left for the Ohio side, so the boys were able to walk all the way to the City Park along the water's edge.

"Hey, has anybody seen General Jackson?" asked Eep.

"Come to think of it, I haven't seen him since all the fuss began," said Wart.

General Stonewall Jackson stood three feet tall and weighed almost seventy pounds. Everyone guessed him to be part Golden Labrador Retriever because of his yellowish blonde coat and love of the water. What other kind of dog he might be was anyone's guess.

"Look, there he is," said Tooth, pointing at the yellow head bobbing along in the river.

"Come here, General. Come on, boy," yelled Eep.

The General loved to swim and the river was his favorite place. He would swim with the boys when they were in the river. The only time he couldn't go with them was when they swam all the way across the river and back.

"I guess he must have jumped in when we did and stayed in waiting for us to come and get him," said Eep.

The big yellow dog walked up out of the water and began shaking all over. The water flew everywhere, creating a small rainstorm.

As he finished shaking, the General began sneezing. One sneeze after another kept coming until finally one last giant sneeze erupted from the dog.

"Oh, yuk. What is that?" asked Tank, looking down at a large slimy patch of goo on his shirt.

"I think it's dog snot and you've got it all over you," laughed Eep.

"Moe, I'm going to kill your brother."

Chapter Five

♣—Finding no trace of the body, the boys' attention was diverted to the large truck pulling into the City Park. It had **HARDY BROTHER'S SHOWS** written in large red letters on the side.

"Hey, the circus starts tomorrow. I'd forgotten all about it," said Dill.

"Yeah, the End Of Summer Festival is this weekend," Wart piped up.

"You know what that means, don't you?" asked Tank.

"School starts next Tuesday," said Tooth.

"Let's go over and see what's going on," Moe suggested.

As the boys walked across the baseball field they had played on all summer, Tank pretended to pitch to Wart. Wart scooped up the invisible ball and yelled for Tooth to cover third base. An exaggerated throw from Wart and a sweeping tag from Tooth sent all the boys into a cheer.

"It's too bad baseball season is over," said Dill. "It's my favorite sport."

"Football season starts next Friday night," Wart said. "That's my favorite sport."

"I know and I like football, but baseball is different," Dill replied. "I just like it better."

The boys had reached the big circus truck when a small man with a funny looking yellow hat came walking around the front of the big rig.

"You boys looking for something?" said the man with the yellow hat.

"No, sir," said Moe. "We just saw your truck and wondered where the rest of the circus was."

"The truck behind me had a wreck above town. The road is blocked by a giant rock that fell right after I went by," said yellow hat. "I came on, but the rest of the trucks are going to be late getting in, so there won't be any show tonight."

"Thanks," said Moe, as the boys turned to walk away.

"Hey, would you boys be interested in earning free passes to the circus?"

"Sure," they all said together.

"Well, if you're here at seven-thirty in the morning, we've got jobs that can earn you a free ticket."

"Thanks, mister. Thanks a lot," said Moe.

"Hey, that was cool," said Wart. "We can work at the circus and they'll give us free passes to get in."

"I would've worked for nothing, if he'd asked," said Tooth.

"Me too," said Dill.

"Me too, but I'll take the tickets," said Tank.

"Listen, they're going to shut down most of the park while they set up the rides," said Moe. "Why don't we follow the river down to Fullcross Island?

Who knows, maybe we might see the body again."

All the River Rats agreed that that sounded like a good idea, so they kept heading south along the riverbank, towards the small island a short distance below the City Park.

Reaching Clear Creek, which emptied into the Ohio River just north of Fullcross Island, the boys could see several pieces of large heavy construction equipment sitting along an empty field beside the river.

"What's all the equipment for?" asked Tank. "Anyone know what's going on?"

They looked back and forth at each other, but no one seemed to have any idea why the equipment might be there.

"Let's go find out what they're doing," said Tank.

"Do you think we ought to get home before Chief Todd talks to our parents?" asked Wart. "It's almost lunch time and they might get worried or maybe get mad that we didn't tell them about what happened."

"Yeah, you're probably right. Maybe we better get home before he shows up and our parents get worried or something," said Dill. "Let's go."

"Wait a minute," said Moe. "I almost forgot. Lucy Hampton's parents have invited us all over to their house for a cookout this afternoon. Her cousins from Oklahoma came in last night and are staying for the weekend. We're supposed to be there at four o'clock."

"Oh, man, do we have to go to Lucy's house?" asked Eep.

"The rest of us are going. You can stay home," said Moe.

"Oh no, if you guys are going, I'm going."

"Hey," said Tooth. "What about all that equipment?"

"Yeah, I think we should find out what's going on over there," said Dill.

"Why don't we come back down here tomorrow?" said Moe. "If no one finds it first, we can come down along the river and look for the body on the way."

"Then we can find out what's going on with all that heavy equipment," Dill said.

They agreed that this sounded like a good plan. All the boys lived within a couple of blocks of each other, in the north end of Monley, so the group made an about-face and headed back in the direction they had come.

Chapter Six

❧—"I don't know why you don't believe me, Elmer," Maye Vern said, looking up at the ceiling. "I saw a ghost and it tried to speak to me. It did. I swear it did."

Seated beside Maye Vern Wheatly's bed at the Monley General Hospital, Chief Todd began to question her about the events at the boat dock.

"Maye Vern, listen. I believe you. I truly do. But, sometimes things aren't exactly what we think they are," Chief Todd explained. His voice was low and consoling. Trying to keep Maye Vern from falling apart again seemed like an impossible task. "Why don't you start from the very beginning?"

"What do you want to know--about the day I was born?" she asked, her voice quivering and becoming very high pitched.

She was getting agitated and Chief Todd knew he would have to handle this situation delicately or Maye Vern might fall apart completely.

"No, Maye Vern. Please. Why don't you start when you and Cal drove over to the Yacht Club."

"Oh. Okay. I can do that," she said, her voice barely above a whisper. "Calmus wanted to get out on the river early. He thought we might have a picnic up on Big Sand Island. After that we planned to go over to Brian's Landing and get some ice cream at the Tastee Freeze."

She stopped for a moment, seeming to collect her thoughts before she started again.

"Elmer, it was a face that came up out of the water. I saw the face of a young man. His eyes were wide open and his mouth moved up and down. It wasn't a ghost. It was real."

Maye Vern began to sob uncontrollably as Calmus wrapped his arms around her.

"I think she's had enough, Elmer," Calmus said.

"No, wait a minute. There's something else." Despite her sobbing, Maye Vern sat straight up in bed. "There was something strange about his face. That's all I can remember, Elmer."

Lying back down on the bed, the tears rolled down her cheeks as she muffled her sobs with a handkerchief.

Calmus looked at the Police Chief. "I think we had better let her rest. I don't think there's anything else she can add."

"She's been a great help. Cal. Please give her a hug for me and my thanks."

Chief Todd's mind began working overtime. He was much older now, but before a shoot-out with bank robbers years earlier he had been a member of an elite FBI squad, and he had been one of their best special field agents. A bullet to the knee had ended his FBI career, but it had not diminished his problem-solving ability. He had an uncanny ability to dissect any situation into its component parts. Finding answers for each eventually resulted in solving the problem.

He was now fairly certain that a body, not a ghost, existed somewhere in the muddy Ohio River somewhere close to Monley. Also, there was something strange about the face of the body. He would need to find it before something else happened.

Al Dristen would be the next person he needed to talk to. He wasn't looking forward to listening to more of Al's tall tales, but if he were going to find out what was going on, he'd have to visit Al.

As the Chief drove away, he didn't see the ambulance pulling up to the hospital's emergency room entrance nor the State Police car that pulled up behind it.

Chapter Seven

❖ Back in his office, Chief of Police Todd rummaged through the little phone number directory on his desk. Not finding what he wanted, he shouted into the adjoining office, "Bobby, get the Marine Patrol people on the phone."

"What's up, Chief?"

"Don't ask any questions, just get them on the phone."

His time with Al Dristen had gone worse than he'd expected. Al had described the body of a huge ugly man floating in the river, which he speculated might be one of the West Virginia Mountain Men.

The Mountain Men were the local legendary Big Foot creatures of the area. Sightings were reported every once in a while, but nothing ever came of them. On one occasion the sighting turned out to be a bull that had some how gotten loose and scared a group of night-hiking Girl Scouts.

The people of Monley still laughed when someone brought up the incident of the night the parachutist got caught in Judge Colter's magnolia tree and how his next-door neighbor Al Dristen had run around snapping pictures and screaming, "It's a Mountain Man. It's a Mountain Man."

In their conversation that afternoon, Al had insisted that there was a connection between what had happened at the boat dock and the Mountain Men. He was sure of it.

"Marine Patrol on the phone, Chief," said Bobby, breaking Chief Todd's train of thought. "It's a guy named Johnson."

"Hello, this is Chief Todd of the Monley Police Department," the Chief said, using his official voice. "Who am I speaking to?"

The conversation went on for a few minutes until the Chief finally finished. "Thanks, we'll be looking for you."

The Marine Patrol would be sending a boat down from Haverville to patrol the area. They had also called ahead to the Yacht Club asking for any boaters to come out and help. Within an hour, seven boats were patrolling the banks of the Ohio River along Monley's riverfront area.

Chapter Eight

❧—When they got home, the boys explained the events at the river to their parents. All the parents felt their sons had acted appropriately and commended them on their quick thinking and unfaltering willingness to help.

"Mom, Lucy's parents have invited all the guys over for a cookout at their house," Dill said.

"Yeah, Moe said we were all invited. Even Eep," Tooth added.

"Well, I guess Dad and I will have to have a quiet dinner alone tonight," said Mrs. Simmons. "Why are the Hamptons inviting all you hooligans over for dinner?"

"Moe said a bunch of Lucy Hampton's cousins are in town for a visit," said Dill.

"That must be Lucy's mother's sister from

Oklahoma and her family," Mrs. Simmons said with a smile.

"If you're going to be alone, where's Sissy going to be?" asked Tooth.

"She's going over to Grandma's for the night. I think she and Grandpa are going to take her to the new Disney movie at the drive-in. What time are you supposed be at the Hamptons?"

"About four-thirty," said Tooth. "But we'll probably go by and pick up Moe and Eep on the way."

"Well, that sounds like fun, but I don't want you playing near the railroad tracks," said their mother. "Do you hear me?"

"But, Mom--" said Dill.

"No buts. No playing by the railroad tracks. One of these days someone is going to get hurt."

Knowing what was coming next, Tooth stepped behind his mother and mouthed her next sentence as she spoke it.

"Someone is going to get sucked under a train and get their legs cut off like Bill Jory," she said, with Tooth mimicking her.

Dill could barely keep a straight face. His mother was always telling the boys about Bill Jory and what had happened when he tried to jump onto a slow moving train. He lost his grip, fell under the train and lost both his legs at the knees. Now he made his way around town in a motorized wheelchair.

"Yes, ma'am, we'll be careful," said Dill.

"Yes, ma'am," said Tooth.

"Listen, you two, if you don't have anything better to do, your father would appreciate it if you'd wash the car."

"Can we drive it?" asked Dill.

"No."

"Is no all you can say?" asked Dill.

"No, I can say you're going to stay home this evening with Dad and me. I could also say that we're going to skip your allowances this week."

"Mom, that's not funny. Besides, today is allowance day. Thanks for reminding us."

Each boy received an allowance every week and for it they were supposed to empty the garbage, after usually being reminded, wash the family's Chihuahua at least every other week and mow the yard in the summer and shovel the snow off the walk in the winter. Their grandparents usually augmented their income. The only requirement for doubling their allowance was to show up once or twice a week and give their grandmother a hug. Once in a while she or their grandfather would ask them to help move furniture, which they were constantly rearranging.

By three-thirty Tooth and Dill were out of things to do at home, so, dressed in clean shorts and tee shirts, they decided to walk over to Moe and Eep's house on the way to Lucy's party.

The boys only lived a block from each other,

so it didn't take long before they were knocking on the back door of the Pitman house.

Eep answered the door. "What do you want?"

Paying no attention to his question, they walked past Eep as if he didn't exist. Moe stood in the middle of the kitchen holding his new Daisy BB gun.

"Do you guys want to go down to the shooting range? We can shoot a few targets before it's time to go to Lucy's house," Moe said.

"Do wild bears squat in the woods? Is a pig's butt pork? Is the Pope a Catholic?" asked Tooth.

"Okay then," said Moe. "Mom and Dad left for the grocery store about fifteen minutes ago, so they won't be back for at least an hour. We've got a few minutes before we're supposed to be at the Hamptons' house, so let's get going."

"What about the pigs and bears and the Pope?" asked Eep. "I don't understand."

Heading out the back door, the boys jumped

off the end of the porch. Halfway down one side of the house was an opening to the crawl space that led under the house. The opening stood barely a foot high and two feet wide, but it was big enough for them to crawl through. Under the house, the crawl space opened up to eighteen inches high.

The house sat on concrete blocks set in rows four feet wide. Over the years, the boys had built a shooting range under the house. By excavating some of the dirt from around the underside of the house, they had built a dirt wall where the BBs would eventually hit behind the targets. That way they could sift through the dirt and recover the BBs, saving them from always having to buy more.

Overhead Moe had designed a pulley system that could retrieve the targets for scoring. He had modeled it after a shooting gallery he had seen in a magazine. There were racks for the extra BB guns that the boys sometimes brought under the house. That way they wouldn't have to lay them in the dirt while they waited their turn to shoot.

Moe had even developed a scoring chart, so they could have shooting matches. Over the last year, the boys had become very proficient with their BB guns.

The clock they kept under the house told them it was now almost four-thirty and they had better be getting over to the Hamptons' for dinner.

Crawling out from under the house, they began beating their shirts and shorts, which made a small dust storm. Luckily none of them had collected too much dirt. Once Moe returned the BB gun to the house, they started off for Lucy Hampton's party.

Chapter Nine

❧—"Hello, boys," came the booming voice of Jim Hampton. He stood six feet six inches tall, and his voice always seemed to be coming from deep inside the big man.

Stories, almost legends, surrounded Jim's basketball days at Monley High School when as a senior he had led the state in scoring and rebounding. The team finished undefeated during the regular season with twenty-two wins and seemed to be a shoo-in for the state title that year. In the championship game of the state playoffs, Monley was leading a team from down state by fifteen points at the start of the fourth quarter, when Jim came down after grabbing a rebound and landed funny on his ankle. At first everyone, including Jim, thought he had just twisted or at worst sprained it.

As he left the game, he thought he would shake it off and return in a few minutes. It turned out that he had torn his Achilles tendon and would never play organized basketball again.

He went off to college, but his heart was no longer in it, so he came home and married his high school sweetheart and went to work in the aluminum mill like so many other men of the area.

"We're having hot dogs and hamburgers," he said. "Which do you want?" He hardly waited for an answer, as he knew they would all eat some of both.

As the boys milled around, Tank and Wart showed up. Lucy must have been waiting for the River Rats to arrive, because as soon as they were all there she came out the back door of the Hampton's house carrying a tray of assorted vegetables and dips. Following her was the most beautiful girl the boys had ever seen. The tall blonde with shoulder-length hair was wearing white shorts and a dark blue tank top. She walked across the patio towards the boys carrying a big bowl of fruit. The River Rats were staring so intently that they hardly noticed the young man about their age following the golden-haired goddess.

Only Dill saw the last person to appear through the patio door. The small girl with light brown hair appeared wearing black short shorts and a light blue tank top. As she smiled, Dill could see the braces she was trying to hide.

Dill walked over to her and asked if he could help carry the large platter of hot dogs and hamburgers she was holding.

"My name is Dill. Can I help with that?"

"No, that's okay. I'm just going to set it on the table," she said, setting the platter down. "My name's Denise, but everyone calls me Deanie."

The other boys were still busy trying to get close to the blonde goddess. Each was trying to say or do something that would catch her attention.

Finally, Tank pushed through the crowd of boys and reached out to take the bowl of fruit from her and said, "Let me take that. It looks heavy." Setting the bowl down he looked at the blonde-haired girl and continued "My name's Tank. Is there anything else I can do for you?"

"Tank, huh. Is that your real name?" she asked.

"Well, it's really Jessie Mathas, but everyone pretty much calls me Tank. What's your name?"

"Alexis. Alexis Smith and this is my twin brother Beauregard," she said, smiling and looking at the boy who had walked up beside her.

"Call me Beau. My sister loves it when she gets to tell everyone my real name," he said.

Beau, though not as heavy, stood almost as tall as Tank. The two eyeballed each other for a minute until finally each broke into big smiles as Tank stuck out his hand. Beau responded by shaking it vigorously.

"Hey. What about me?" asked Alexis.

"Would you like something to drink?" asked Tank.

"A Coke would be fine."

For the next two hours the boys got to know Lucy's cousins a lot better.

Tank and Alexis sat under the maple tree at the far end of the Hampton's yard. Dill and Deanie sat at the picnic table talking about school and how they wished the summer was longer and the school year shorter.

The rest of the River Rats and Beau had convinced Jim that they should play a little basketball. Jim still liked to shoot a few hoops, so he had put up a goal on the end of his garage. The boys, minus Tank and Dill, chose up sides and began playing after dinner.

"What is there to do in this podunk town?" asked Beau.

"Would any of you boys like to tell Beau about our podunk town or should I?" responded Jim.

When none of the boys took Jim up on his offer, he said, "Have a seat. I think there are quite a few similarities between Tulsa and Monley."

"Wait a minute, Uncle Jim," said Beau. "Are you going to try and tell me that this little burg is somehow like Tulsa?"

"Yeah, that's exactly what I'm saying. Let me begin at the beginning and maybe you'll understand...."

Chapter Ten

◆—The wind roared out of the west whipping waves on the river to a height of over three feet. A storm like this only came along once in a lifetime, and today, in the year 1789, young Captain Richard Wheatly kept fighting to keep his flat boat from slamming against the rocks along the river's banks. The waves poured over the sides of the small boat and he knew it wouldn't last much longer if he didn't find a place to land.

Seeing a large creek that appeared to offer shelter, he guided the boat towards the cove and potential safety. Barely fifty feet from the mouth of the creek, a large wave tossed the boat sideways into a sandbar hidden under the water. The front end of the boat immediately caved in, throwing Richard Wheatly into the stormy waters of the

Ohio River.

Finally crawling ashore, he began rescuing as much of his provisions as he could. He returned to the storm-tossed river many times until he could no longer stand. Collapsing on the embankment exhausted, he slept through the rest of the storm.

The sun peeking through the large grove of maple trees awakened Captain Wheatly. He immediately jumped up and began to go through the goods he had brought ashore the previous evening. As he began going through the remnants of his possessions, he could see the sandbar that his boat had slammed against the previous evening. It went on for several hundred yards, before it widened to become a small island in the river. His boat, or the remnants of it, were scattered along the banks of the island. He was only a few hundred feet from the shore, so after collecting all the provisions and pieces of his boat he could find he set out to explore the area.

Venturing up the embankment, he discovered a mile-long plateau fifty feet above the river's edge. As he explored, he found that from the edge of the plateau to the edge of the three hills surrounding it, an area half a mile wide and little over a mile long existed. Plenty of trees existed to use for building material and enough land could be cleared to raise crops and animals.

Over the next few days he set up stone markers every five hundred yards around the whole plateau. Along the stream at the north end of the plateau, he took the remnants of his flat boat and built a small lean-to shack. For a month he hunted, trapped and explored the area around his claim. Finding no identifying markers, he decided this would be the end of the line for him. Here he would build his future.

Twenty-eight year old Captain Richard Wheatly, late of the first New Jersey Militia, found the home he had been searching for. One year later he brought his bride, Sarah Monley, to this wilderness outpost. By that time, he had cleared almost fifty acres and had built a small combination house and store. He'd hung a sign at the river's edge – Fresh Water and Provisions TOP OF THE HILL.

With those words, the beginning of a town had begun. Richard Wheatly, Captain in the American Revolutionary War, had now become a gentleman farmer and tradesman. With seventy-five hundred acres claimed and registered in the Virginia land office, Richard and Sarah Monley Wheatly would give birth to a town. Richard so adored his wife that he named the settlement, Monley, after her family name.

They would raise fifteen children on this land, eight boys and seven girls. A school would be started as more residents arrived. Coal, oil and natural gas would be discovered on and around the area settled by the Wheatly family. A boom town of nearly twenty thousand would exist for a short period at the beginning of the 20th century, but by the 1950s, only a few thousand people would inhabit Monley. Still, it retained most of the grace and charm of that bygone era.

* * *

Calmus Richard Wheatly was the last living descendant of the original settler still living in Monley. Along with his wife, Maye Vern, he tried to keep the traditions of the past alive in this small town in what had become the state of West Virginia in 1863, during the Civil War.

"But where did all the people go, if there used to be twenty thousand of them here?" asked Beau.

"Oh, they followed the oil west to places in Kentucky, Indiana, Missouri and Oklahoma," said Jim. "That's how your grandfather ended up in Oklahoma. He was an oil field worker that just moved to where the oil took him."

"And all the oil wells, where are they?"

"Any of you boys want to tell him where the wells are?"

"Underground," said Moe. "They've all been either capped in, or are being pumped from one pumping station. There used to be an oil derrick in my back yard, but they took it down a couple of years ago."

"There are still several oil company headquarters in town," Tooth added.

"We've even got an opera house," said Eep. "But it's a hardware store now."

"It's almost seven. If we're going to make it to the movie on time, we're going to have to leave pretty soon. Why don't you guys go to the movie with us and we can show you some of those places on the way downtown," Moe said, looking at Beau and his sisters.

"I think that's a great idea," said Jim.

After a quick discussion with their parents and a stern warning about coming right home after

the movie, the group took off towards downtown
Monley and the Paramount Theatre.

Chapter Eleven

❖—It was almost ten o'clock when the movie ended. The group headed toward the north end of town when suddenly Tooth stopped and said, "Beau, I dare you to touch the door in Dead-Man's alley.

"What?" said Beau.

"Tooth just dared you to touch the door at the back of Dead-Man's alley," said Eep. "You're not a chicken, are you?"

"What door and what dead man?" Beau asked.

"See that alleyway two doors up?" asked Moe.

"Yeah."

"Well, you have to walk all the way to the back of the alley and touch the door where there's a little light shining inside," Moe explained.

"That doesn't sound too hard," said Beau.

"Well, you have to walk back to the door. You can't run, but once you've touched the door then you have to try to catch up to the rest of us. If you catch any of us before we cross the railroad tracks, then you get a free shot on the guy who dared you."

"A free shot?" Beau didn't understand what Moe meant.

"You get to hit him in the arm as hard as you can, but only if you catch up to at least one of the group."

"Okay, but what about the dead man?"

"A long time ago, a man was found dead in the alley and now people say the alley is haunted."

"Oh, great, it's a haunted alley."

"Be sure to touch the back door in the alley or the ghost will come after you. That's what people say."

As Beau started down the alley, he turned to see several of the group were already gone. A few feet later he was totally engulfed in darkness. He could barely see the tiny light shining through the door at the end of the alley. He kept walking and began a very low whistle as he walked. Finally a few feet from the door, he jumped forward, touched the door and began running back towards the lighted street.

Halfway back out of the alley, he tripped over something that hadn't been there when he walked in. Jumping to his feet, he ran like the Devil was chasing him. Actually at that moment, Beau thought the Devil or at least a ghost was chasing him.

As he ran out of the alley, he rounded the corner and could see the rest of the group a full block ahead of him. Now all he wanted to do was to catch any of them before they reached the railroad tracks. He wanted revenge on Tooth for daring him to walk down Dead-Man's alley.

His legs felt like lead and he already had a

sharp pain in his side as he reached the end of the first block. His only hope was to catch one of his sisters. He knew he could never catch any of the River Rats.

Tank and Alexis had taken off early, so Beau had no chance of catching them. Dill and Deanie had waited around until they could no longer see Beau in the alley before they had taken off running.

Beau continued to run as fast as he could, but the pain in his side kept slowing him down. Dill and Deanie were less than a half-block ahead, but still had over a block to go before they reached the railroad tracks.

Tooth had already reached the tracks and yelled at his brother to hurry up. "Drag her if you have to, but don't let Beau catch up."

Dill and Deanie were now less that half a block from the tracks, but Beau was catching up quickly. Dill grabbed Deanie's hand and began running faster, pulling her along faster than her legs were actually capable of moving.

"I'm going to fall. I'm going to--"

As Deanie stumbled and began to lose her balance, Dill turned and caught her. He held her upright and allowed her to regain her balance, but Dill wasn't so lucky. He went down with a thud, sliding several feet on the sidewalk. Deanie crossed the railroad tracks, but Dill couldn't quite make it up before Beau passed him.

"Thanks a lot brother," Tooth said, sarcastically.

"I'll trade you my scraped arm for the punch Beau is going to give you," said Dill.

"No. If Deanie hadn't almost fallen, you would have beaten me," said Beau. "Thanks for keeping her from falling."

"You're okay, Beau," said Tooth.

"Yeah, you are definitely okay. How'd you like to be a River Rat?" asked Moe.

"Sure," said Beau.

"Well, you've already passed the first test to be a River Rat."

"What's that?"

"You walked back Dead-Man's alley," said Wart.

"What else do I have to do?"

"We'll show you tomorrow," said Moe.

As they reached the Hampton house, the boys began to go their separate ways. Tank and Alexis walked up towards the front porch, while Dill and Deanie stood on the street corner. After a couple of minutes a very low voice came out of the darkness of the Hamptons' porch.

"It's time for you all to come on in."

The boys knew instantly it was Jim Hampton's voice.

"Yes, sir. We'll be right there."

The rest of the group said goodnight and headed for home.

Moe turned and hollered at Beau. "Do you

want to go with us in the morning? We're going down to the park to see if we can get free passes for the circus."

"Sure. What time."

"I'll pick you up at seven."

"See you then," said Beau. "Oh, can the girls come?"

"No, not this time. You'll see why tomorrow."

Chapter Twelve

❧ "Hey, where's Wart?" Moe asked.

Looking around at the collected group, Tank said, "It ain't my week to watch him."

"Yeah, but you guys usually always come together."

"Well, if he's not here, then tough. He doesn't get a free ticket. You snooze, you lose."

Moe looked at his watch. The group would barely have time to make it to the park before seven-thirty. They would definitely be late if they waited for Wart to show up.

"Dill, go check on Wart. We'll head for the park. We'll tell them you're on your way."

The group turned and headed for the park as Dill ran as fast as he could towards Wart's house.

"Yes, sir. I know we said there would be six of

us," Moe began explaining to the short man with the wrinkled face. "Wait a minute, here come the other two now."

"Now you've got seven."

"We brought along another friend. I hope that's okay," Moe said.

"If your friend doesn't care, we've got plenty for you to do. Amos, put these boys to work."

A huge man who smelled like he had just crawled out from under an outhouse waved his hand for the group to follow him. They walked around the large tent that had been put up on the park grounds the night before. Looking around, the River Rats could see large tractor-trailer trucks parked in rows near the creek that flowed through the park. They seemed to be walking toward these trucks, but what kind of work could they do around a group of tractor-trailer trucks?

Each boy imagined being at the wheel of the big trucks. What fun it would be driving down the road in one of these big rigs, blasting away on the loud air-horn, scaring old ladies and little kids.

Moe, being the most practical of the group, thought they might get a job washing the trucks. There were several of them, and that seemed to be an awful big job for a one-day free pass to the carnival and circus.

As they came closer to the trucks, the big smelly man began to walk around the trucks. Without saying a word and using only hand signals, he directed the boys to continue following him as he passed the outside of the last truck.

To the boys' surprise, there behind the trucks, next to the creek, stood a large tent with three elephants, a camel and a cage with a tiger in it.

Their imaginations began conjuring up all kinds of scenarios for what they would be doing for the next few hours.

Moe imagined walking the animals on big leashes.

Tank pictured himself watering the animals.

Wart imagined throwing raw meat to lions, tigers or bears. Maybe one of them would eat Eep.

Eep imagined himself on top of an elephant, walking through downtown Monley.

A voice broke them out of their dreams. "You two big fellows follow me. The rest of you put on a pair of those waders over there."

The smelly man had spoken and now pointed to Tank and Moe to follow him. "I'll be back in a minute. The rest of you get your boots on."

Moe and Tank waved as they walked out of the tent. The rest of the River Rats, including their newest member, Beau, put on the large rubber boots, which they found they could put on right over their tennis shoes.

In a couple of minutes the large man returned. He waved for them to follow him, which they did with more than a little difficulty. The boots were so big that the boys' feet slid back and forth inside them as they walked. The man didn't slow down to wait for them, so they had to keep up as best they could.

Finally reaching the other side of the tent, it dawned on each of them what their job would be.

In front of them stood several large mounds of poop. The elephants and camel must have been running constantly since they arrived to have created such enormously large piles. The carnival workers had cleaned out the inside of the tent where the animals were kept, but the River Rats' job would be to move it somewhere else. But where and how was the question.

"Hey. Guys," Moe hollered.

The five pooper-scoopers looked up to see Moe and Tank unloading hay at the far edge of the animal tent.

"I guess you guys got the soft job," he said, laughing.

Tank could barely catch his breath as he bent over laughing. The five scoopers could see the tears streaming down his face as he held his sides trying to keep from laughing.

"If you two can't keep busy, you can join your buddies," said Amos.

"Yes, sir," they said in unison.

For the next two and a half hours all seven of them worked as they had never worked before. Moe and Tank moved a hundred bales of hay, while the other five, using pitchforks, shovels and wheelbarrows, moved more poop than a single get-in-free ticket was worth. They moved the smelly piles from the edge of the animal tent to the two large dump trucks that had backed up along the back of the animal tent. The trucks would then carry their loads of poop off to some place faraway.

Once they started, none of them dared quit. The other River Rats would never let them live it down, so they spent their two and a half hours shoveling and gagging, wheeling and gagging, and dumping and gagging.

Eep stopped twice to hurl his breakfast. By the time they finished, his face looked as white as a sheet and he was gasping for breath.

When the last wheelbarrow load had been dumped, the smelly man showed up right on time.

"Don't take your boots off just yet," he said.

Oh no, the boys thought. Could there be another tent?

But to their surprise, he showed them where they could rinse off their boots and wash up.

"Line your boots up over there where you got them and follow me."

Moe and Tank showed up as the other five were taking off their boots. They all then proceeded to follow Amos back towards the front of the circus.

"They did a good job, Duke. I think you should pay them."

"All right, boys. Let's see. I owe each of you a

free pass to the circus. Is that right?" asked Duke, who had greeted them that morning. They hadn't seen him since, but they had heard Amos mention the boss several times.

"Yes, sir," all the River Rats said together.

"Well, Amos says you did a fairly good job. You two moved more hay than any group we've ever had work for us, and the rest of you moved a pretty good load of manure. I think maybe we should change the terms of our agreement," he said, reaching into his back pocket.

The boys had no idea what the wrinkled man was up to.

"Here are your passes for the afternoon circus performance and here are passes for the carnival midway rides. Does that sound fair?"

"Yeah."

"Sure."

"That's great."

They were all talking at once, but they were

all happy that they had stuck with the job that morning.

"Here's a piece of advice that I'd like for each of you to think about. If you don't finish school, what you were doing this morning may be what you'll be doing the rest of your life. Now, I think you might want to get on home and take a bath," Duke said, laughing. "We'll see you at the circus."

He turned and walked off around the end of the tent and disappeared behind one of the tractor-trailer trucks.

"Let's get out of here," Moe said.

With that, the boys took off towards the north end of the park and the road along the river that led towards home.

"You know," said Dill. "I'm glad baseball season is over."

"Why?"asked Wart. "I thought you loved baseball."

"I do, but some of that poop is going to be in the outfield for a long time."

Chapter Thirteen

❧—"Look," said Wart. "The Marine Patrol is looking for the body."

"It's long gone by now," said Tooth.

"What body?" asked Beau. "First you've got Dead-Man's alley and now a body in the river."

"Well, we sort of ran into it yesterday," said Moe, as he began telling Beau about the couple they had helped rescue from the water and how Tooth had seen what he thought was a body.

"You guys are in the middle of everything around here. I'm glad I made the trip this summer."

As the boys walked along the river, they kept watching the small boats driving against the strong current of the river. The nets the boats trailed behind made it almost impossible for them to keep going in a straight line.

Suddenly they heard an excited cry from one of the boats near the ferryboat landing.

"We've got something," one man ex-claimed. "It seems pretty heavy. We're going to need some help."

The boat turned towards shore, but between the current and whatever had been trapped in the net, they were being drawn backwards. Finally a second boat arrived at their side and threw a rope to help pull them towards shore.

They had just about reached the shore when one of the men in the first boat stood up to throw a rope to one of the men on the bank. As he let go of the rope, the boat suddenly lurched forward, toppling the man backward into the dark gurgling water.

A lady on shore screamed as the man fell overboard. All the other boats pulled in their nets and began circling towards where the man had fallen into the water. After a few seconds his head popped up about twenty feet down stream from where he had fallen in. Ropes from two different boats were thrown towards him, but both failed to land within his reach.

Finally one of the Marine Patrol boats came alongside the man and extended an oar to him. Within a minute, he sat safely in the rescue boat smiling and waving to the people who had gathered on the bank.

Excitement filled the air, but still no trace of the elusive body.

Chief Todd stood on the bank watching everything that was happening. His face gave no indication of what he might be thinking, but inside, his mind worked overtime.

If a body really existed, why couldn't it have been found? If Maye Vern hadn't seen a body, what did she see? Finally, he thought, what could he be missing? Had he overlooked anything? Maybe he needed to talk to that group of boys who had been there when it all started. What did they call themselves? Oh yeah, the River Rats.

As the excitement began to subside, the River Rats were at the north end of the park heading for home. Chief Todd, standing along the bank at the south end of the park, began a leisurely stroll back to his patrol car.

Neither the boys nor Chief Todd noticed the piece of rope caught up under the ferryboat, Big Moses, as it left the West Virginia side to make its umpteenth trip to Ohio that day. Barely visible, if anyone had been looking from along the bank, and totally out of sight from anyone on board the ferry, the additional passenger with red eyes continued to ride back and forth across the river under the ferryboat.

Chapter Fourteen

❧—River Boulevard ran true to its name. The wide brick street ran directly along the river's edge. Ahead of him, Chief Todd could see the seven boys walking along in the light rain that had just begun to fall.

They don't have a care in the world, he thought, as he pulled up beside them and rolled down his window.

"Can I give you boys a lift home?"

"Nah, that's okay, Chief. We're almost there," Moe said.

"Come on. I need to ask you a couple of questions. You might as well stay dry while we're talking."

Chief Todd cringed as the boys jumped into the car. They were soaking wet and more than a little dirty and smelly.

"You boys remember the other day when Calmus and Maye Vern Wheatly fell into the river?" he asked.

"Sure. Why?" asked Tank.

"Well, it seems that Mrs. Wheatly is convinced that she saw something. That in fact, it was a body of a young man. Did any of you see anything? I mean anything at all?"

"No. sir," said Moe.

"How about any of the rest of you?" Chief Todd asked.

They all shook their heads no except Tooth. He looked out the window away from Chief Todd.

In his years with the FBI, Chief Todd had learned to spot when someone was holding back information. Without wanting to put the boys on the spot, he kept the conversation going.

"You know, if someone did see something, the right thing to do would be to let us know. That way we might have a better chance of finding out who or what Mrs. Wheatly saw in the river. It could be that somebody's parents might be looking for them and we wouldn't know they were missing."

The silence inside the car gave it the feeling of a tomb. Each of the boys kept looking around, wishing they were somewhere else.

The Chief let them sit there in silence for a couple of minutes before he reached down to start the car.

"If it were one of you out there, I'm sure your mama would want to know," he said.

"Chief," Tooth said, hesitantly.

"Yes, son."

"Maybe I saw something, but I don't know for sure. I don't know if it would be of any help or not."

"Why don't you tell me and I'll be the judge of whether it can help or not."

"When we were pulling the boat in to shore that

day, as I looked back, I thought I saw something. It could have been a man's back. Or it might have been a log. I only saw it for a second. I'm sorry. Does that help?"

"Well, it's a start. It's more than I knew an hour ago. Is there anything else?"

"No, sir."

"What about the rope?" Moe said.

"What rope?" Chief Todd asked.

"Oh, I almost forgot," said Tooth. "Just before whatever it was slipped under the water, it looked like there was a rope tied around it. It looked kind of funny."

"Funny how?" asked the Chief.

"I'm not sure. It happened so fast, but it just looked funny," Tooth said.

Chief Todd pulled up to Moe's house to let the boys out.

"Listen, if you boys think of anything else, call me."

"Maybe we can help," said Moe. "We're all good swimmers and no one knows the area along the river bank as well as we do."

"You boys have been a big help already, but from here on you leave this to the Police and the Marine Patrol."

The police car drove off down the block leaving the boys standing in the rain outside of Moe's house.

"I think we can find that body," said Moe.

"Yeah, I think we can too," said his little brother.

"Shut up, you little twerp. What do you know?" said Tank.

"I know you're a big doofus," said Eep.

"Moe, I swear, one of these days I'm going to whack him good," said Tank.

"Ah, leave him alone. Besides, we've got other things to do. We've got a body to find."

"What we need is a plan," said Moe.

"What we need is to get out of the rain," said Wart.

The boys moved up onto Moe's back porch. Sitting there watching the rain, no one spoke for several minutes.

"Right now let's get cleaned up and meet back here at one-thirty. The afternoon circus performance starts at two o'clock," said Moe.

They all took off heading for home and looking forward to the afternoon.

Driving away, all Chief Todd could think of at the moment was how bad his new car smelled. Those boys must have been playing in the sewer.

Chapter Fifteen

❧—"Whoa. Where do you think you're going, Mr. Buddy?" Dill's mom asked, stopping him at the back door. "You stink to high heaven. And where is Tooth?"

"Right here," said Tooth, coming around the side of the house.

"No. No. No! Neither of you is coming in the house," she said, making a face. "What did you do, fall into a sewage pit?"

"Come on, Mom--"

His mother cut Dill off before he could continue. "You two head over to Grandma's basement. You can take a shower there. I'll bring you a change of clothes."

"But, Mom--"

"No. That's final. You both smell like that

dog when it rolled in the manure pile. What have you been doing? Did you knock over someone's outhouse and fall in? Are you two in trouble? Are the police going to show up on the front steps?"

"No, Mom, I swear. We didn't do any-thing wrong. We've been working at the carnival shoveling elephant poop. We earned a free pass for the circus this afternoon and because we did a good job, we get to ride all the midway rides free ."

"Do you have the passes on you?" she asked.

"Yes, ma'am," they answered.

"Give them over. I'll air them out and you can have them later. Now get over to Grandma's. Throw all your clothes into one of her empty washtubs and don't forget to use plenty of soap, especially on your hair. Now get."

As the other boys got near their house, Moe looked at Eep and said, "You stink. Mom isn't going to be happy if you go in and mess up the bathroom. Why don't you undress on the side porch and I'll hang your clothes out on the line to air out."

"I don't want to undress on the porch. Lucy might see me," Eep answered.

"Listen, if you mess up the bathroom, I'm the one who is going to get in trouble. If I get in trouble, then I'll beat you black and blue. Understand?"

"Okay, but you've got to look out for her."

"Sure, I can do that. Now get going."

Since Tank hadn't worked around the poop, he didn't smell as bad as some of the others. Wart's mom marched him back outside and into the basement where she had him undress and rinse off with the garden hose before taking a bath.

At the Hamptons' place, Beau had a lot of explaining to do, but he ended up in the basement like the rest. Lucy peeked out through the curtains of her bedroom window just as Eep ran into the house wearing nothing but his skivvies.

Chapter Sixteen

◦⟞The elephants led the parade into the big top. This wasn't the three-ring Ringling Brothers Shrine Circus that the boys had seen up in Wheeling, but the one large ring in the center of the tent promised excitement galore for the afternoon performance.

The tickets the River Rats received for working with the animals had assured them of front row seats. The girls had accompanied them and all ten of them now squeezed into seats where only seven should have been sitting. The boys didn't care. The girls smelled a lot better than where they had been that morning.

Deanie's arms flew up as the lead elephant passed by just feet from the group, lowering its head and slowly giving a loud trumpeting sound. Startled, she jumped up, throwing popcorn everywhere.

After the elephant passed, she stood sheepishly not knowing what to do. Sensing her distress, Dill jumped up, throwing his bag of popcorn in the air.

Looking at him, she said, "Are you nuts?"

"No, I just thought you might like some company while you were standing there."

"Sit down, you two," came a voice from behind them. "My kid can't see."

They sat down, still looking at each other. The parade of circus performers continued in front of them, but the Queen of Sheba pulled by seven-headed kangaroos would have passed unnoticed at that moment.

The ring announcer's voice broke the spell.

"Ladies and gentlemen. Children of all ages. Please direct your attention to my immediate left. The fantastic Scarlotta Family direct from their appearance before the crowned heads of Europe will amaze you with their death-defying acrobatics on the high wire. Maestro, if you please."

The band started to play as the three ladies unfurled their capes. Four men stepped to a rope ladder and held it steady as the ladies climbed twenty feet to the high wire. Quickly the men followed. Their performance began with each of them walking out a few feet onto the wire and then returning to the small platform. As two of the men and one lady began walking across the wire, a clown carrying a large wicker basket began following their moves on the ground below. For the next fifteen minutes they crawled over, under and around each other. Sometimes they even had chairs and a table with them.

The climax came when they built a pyramid. Three men were on the bottom holding a table, while the ladies sat on chairs atop the table, having tea. When they began to wobble, the teapot slid off the table as the crowd gasped. The clown below swooped over and caught the teapot in his large basket.

"Hey, that clown would make a pretty good centerfielder," said Tank.

"Better than some people. That's for sure," Wart agreed.

"Give me a break. The sun was in my eyes and you know it. You couldn't have done any better," said Dill, referring to a fly ball he had dropped in a baseball game the previous week.

"Did I say anything about dropping an easy fly ball that let in the winning run?" asked Tank. "Did I?"

"No, you didn't," said Wart. "But I think that guy could've caught it."

The good-natured ribbing went on the rest of the show until they brought the elephants back out.

"Ladies and gentlemen. The piece d'resistance. The one. The only. Colonel Markham T. Pangborn's Amazing Pachyderms."

With that, the curtain on the far side of the tent opened and out ran two large elephants. Using his trunk, a baby elephant held onto the tail of the second large elephant in front of him.

Atop the first elephant rode a beautiful lady wearing large red, white and blue feathers that reached at least three feet above her head. She wore what looked like a gold one-piece bathing suit.

Standing on top of the second elephant, a man did flips and hand stands as all three elephants ran around the ring.

The elephants stopped and did a complete circle and then seemed to do a couple of dance moves while the band played music that sounded like it came from the jungle of Africa.

For the next few minutes the huge animals did all kinds of tricks before running out of the center ring and exiting through the doorway they had entered.

"Ladies and gentlemen, we would like four

young volunteers from the audience to assist us."

From kids and a few adults, hands went up all around the tent. The clown that had caught the teapot earlier came running around in front of the seats. He reached in and grabbed Wart and Moe by the hand and had them follow him to the center of the ring. A clown on the far side of the big top had done the same thing and quickly moved towards the center of the ring.

Just then the two large elephants came racing back into the tent. After a couple of quick passes around the outside of the ring, they slowed and the guys with the big sticks, running alongside the elephants, guided them to the center of the ring. They now stood beside the four young men who had been chosen to help with the finale.

As they came to a halt, each of the huge animals rocked back on its hind legs and lifted its front legs. Seeming to paw at the air, the elephants lifted their trunks at the same time and made loud trumpeting sounds.

When the elephants began to trumpet, each of the four boys took a step away. It was an instinctive reaction to something so large that sounded so mean.

Each clown then escorted the two boys they had chosen into the ring. The trainers had the two animals lower their heads halfway down their front legs. Then one boy from each group--Wart from the River Rats--stepped on the elephant's trunk, after which it raised the boy up to its head where the person riding above helped them climb on board the elephant's back.

Moe and the other boy were instructed to lie down on the ground flat on their backs. The trainers then guided each pachyderm to a point beside each boy and instructed the huge beast to raise their foot over the now prone youngsters.

Moe closed his eyes, and the clown knelt beside him saying, "Don't move. I'll tell you when to get up."

Moe wasn't moving. He wasn't even breathing. All he could think of was getting out from under that monstrous foot.

Suddenly, the clown tugged at Moe's arm.

"Get up and smile," the clown said.

Moe jumped up and started to move away, but the clown held a firm grip on his arm. "Smile and raise your arms over your head. You're a hero, son. Smile."

Moe did smile. He raised his arms over his head and did a little dance. Looking up, he caught sight of Wart riding on top of the elephant. Grinning from ear to ear he sat in front of the lady in the gold bathing suit with red, white and blue feathers.

"Ladies and gentlemen. Let's give a big round of applause for our intrepid volunteers."

Moe and the other boy who had lain under an elephant's foot returned to the stands just as the band struck up a John Philip Sousa march.

The trainers led the elephants out of the ring and started to parade past the grandstands as the flaps opened at the far end of the tent and in came all the performers and animals that had been a part of the show that day. Leading the parade atop the first elephant, Wart waved to the crowd as if he were one of the performers. The parade marched two times around the big ring before exiting.

"Ladies and gentlemen. Thank you for coming today. You have been the greatest audience for one of the world's premier circus performances. Please watch your step as you exit and be sure to help the ladies. Also take time to enjoy our midway attractions just outside. Thank you and we hope to see you again real soon."

All of the River Rats and the girls could hardly stop talking. It was complete chaos as each tried to talk louder than the rest.

"What was it like with that big foot over your head?"

"I didn't--" Moe tried to answer, but another question cut him off.

"Did you think it was going to step on you?"

"I didn't--" Again he was interrupted before he could answer.

"Did his feet stink?" asked Eep.

With that question, they all started laughing.

Chapter Seventeen

❧—"Mom," Tooth shouted. "Mom, do you know where my striped shirt is?"

"In your drawer," she replied, standing in the bedroom doorway.

"Sorry. I didn't know you were there."

"Well."

"Well, what?" he asked.

"Is it in your drawer?"

Pulling his top drawer open, he immediately saw the shirt he was looking for.

"Yes, ma'am. I found it, but it wasn't there a minute ago."

"I see. It just appeared there all by itself."

"I guess," Tooth said, sheepishly. "Thanks."

From behind him, Tooth could hear his brother snickering. "You are too easy."

"Did you put that shirt in there?"

"Do wild bears squat in the woods?"

"Don't start with the bears and little animals with me," said Tooth. "I'll knock your lights out."

"You'd have to catch me first and you aren't fast enough," Dill yelled, as he raced past his brother and out the door.

Racing on down the steps and out the front door, he jumped on the tree swing in the front yard and waited for his brother to come flying out of the house after him.

"Hey, where's Tooth?" asked Wart as he rounded the hedges that separated the Simmons' house from the one next door.

"He ought to come flying out the door any minute now."

"I'm going to punch your--" Tooth was yelling, but suddenly changed his mind about what he wanted to say. "Is it time to head for the midway already?"

"Yeah--where's the rest of the guys?"

Moe and Eep showed up with Lucy and her cousins. Tank arrived a few minutes later and the whole group set off for the City Park and an evening at the midway.

As they stepped up to the ticket booth, the boys presented their passes and were immediately given wrist bracelets that would be good to ride any ride as many times as they wanted that evening. If the bracelet was cut off, then it could no longer be used by anyone.

When the girls had paid for their wrist bracelets, the group took off in the direction of the Ferris wheel.

"Would you like to ride on the Ferris wheel?" Wart asked Alexis.

"Sure. Let's go."

Tank gave Wart a dirty stare, but didn't say anything.

Eep headed for the hot dog stand, as the rest of

the group stood in line at the ride. Dill and Deanie were first in line, followed by Wart and Alexis. Lucy looked around for Eep, but he had given her the slip. He knew that if he hung around with the group that he would eventually end up having to ride the Ferris wheel with her and there was no way he was going to let that happen.

As Dill and Deanie settled back into their seat, the ticket-taker closed the bar in front of them.

"I hope we don't fall out," said Dill.

"Do me a favor. Don't rock this thing as we go around. Please," said Deanie.

"Sure. Why, are you afraid?"

As the giant wheel began to move backwards, Deanie grabbed his arm and buried her face into his shoulder.

"Hey, are you all right?"

"No, but I didn't want my brother and sister laughing at me. They think they are so smart because they are a year older. They both give me a hard time, all the time."

"It's okay. We're not going to fall. I've been riding these things since I was a little kid," said Dill. "You just go around in a circle. First you go up and then back down. That's all there is to it."

As the wheel moved again, Deanie peeked out around his shoulder and could see Alexis and Wart in the seat in front of them. She knew that any moment her sister would turn around and laugh at her. Immediately she pulled closer to Dill and held tightly onto his arm. To anyone watching them from the ground, they looked like a boyfriend and girlfriend getting comfortable for a spin on the wheel. Deanie stared straight ahead, not daring to look down as the wheel moved again. This time Tank and Beau got on, followed by Tooth and Moe. Lucy quickly squeezed in between them.

Finally, the wheel was filled with new riders and they began going up the backside of the giant circle clear to the top before they fell down the front side of the wheel's circuit.

"*Aaaaaaaahhhhhheeeeeooooo*," cried Deanie, as she squeezed hard on Dill's arm.

"Are you okay?" he asked.

"Noooo," she moaned, as they floated down from the high point of the wheel.

Starting back up again, she finally lifted her head to look around.

"It's beautiful," she said.

"Yes. It is," he said, looking at her, not at the surroundings.

As they floated down the front side of the circle, she held on to Dill's arm, but not quite as tight this time. She stifled a desire to scream. She made a low sound that only Dill could hear.

Finally the wheel began to slow down. Dill and Deanie were stopped at the very top while the next group of riders began to get on.

"It really is beautiful up here," she said. "Thank you for riding with me and not making fun of me."

"Thank you. I had a great time," said Dill. "Maybe we can ride it again after while."

"I think that would be great," she answered.

The rest of the evening the group rode on the rides, ate all kinds of food, including something hot and sugary called a funnel cake, and played games of chance up and down the midway. At ten-thirty, Deanie looked at Dill and said, "I have to be home by eleven. I'm sorry."

"That's okay. We've ridden everything at least twice. I'm ready to go."

They walked over to the rest of the group. "Deanie has to be home by eleven, so we're going to start back."

"Yeah, I have to be home by eleven also," said Alexis. "And so do you, Beauregard."

"We'd all better start for home," said Moe. "We can come back tomorrow."

All the way, the guys, except for Wart and Dill, raced from block to block. Dill with Deanie, and

Wart with Alexis, each tried to walk slower than the other couple, but they ended up walking on different sides of the street. That way they could talk, but the other two couldn't overhear what they were saying.

When they all finally reached the Green Corner, Moe said, "Are we still going on a bike hike tomorrow?"

"Yeah. We're still going," said Tank. "Why wouldn't we go?"

"Can I go?" asked Deanie.

"Uh. I don't know," said Dill. "We've never had a girl go with us before. We sometimes go ten or even twenty miles out the dirt roads. A lot of them are up and down some pretty big hills."

"I don't think I want to go," she said. "I'm not that much of a biker. Besides, I don't have a bike with me."

Alexis agreed that she wasn't really interested in going on a bike hike either. Lucy, who would have given her next month's allowance to go with the guys, knew any chance she had of ever going along had just evaporated.

"How about you, Beau?" Moe asked. "You want to go?"

"I don't have a bike."

"We'll get you a bike and you can become a real River Rat," said Tank. "There's only one more part to the initiation that you'll have to pass."

"As long as it doesn't involve any ghosts or bodies or anything like that," Beau said.

"Well, you'll have to jump off Dead-Man's Leap," said Eep.

"What? Are you kidding me? Does everything around here have something to do with dead things?"

"Don't worry about it," said Wart. "If Eep could do it, you can do it. We'll show you how and then you can decide if you want to or not."

"Okay, that sounds fair," said Beau. "When do

we leave?"

"Seven-thirty," said Moe. "We'll meet at my house. Everyone be sure to bring a lunch and something to drink."

"Yeah. Tomorrow we're going to see if Beau can fly," said Tooth.

Chapter Eighteen

❧—"I wish something would happen," said Eep.

"You know what Grandma says–Be careful what you wish for, it just might come true," answered his brother Moe.

"I know, but summer's over and we have to go back to school next week. Wouldn't it be cool if something exciting happened?"

"What more do you want to happen? We helped save the Wheatlys. That was pretty cool, I think," said Dill.

"Oh, you know what I mean. Just something," said Eep.

The seven boys pushed their bikes down the railroad tracks in the early morning fog.

"The fog is still pretty thick this morning," said Tooth.

"Yeah, but it's starting to break up," Dill said. "Look, the sun is shining on the tracks up ahead."

The fog still hung in the air like sheets of dirty laundry, but the breeze blowing across the river blew it up the cliff beside the railroad tracks. The sun now peeked through gray mist, lighting up the area around the boys in alternating shades of pale and dark gray.

"Hey, look at that," shouted Eep.

"What?" asked Tank.

"Up there, just below that small tree. That has got to be the biggest hornets' nest in the whole world."

"Where? I don't see anything."

"Well, then, you must be blind," said Eep.

"Moe, one of these days--" exclaimed Tank.

Turning to see what all the racket was about, Moe saw that his younger brother had laid his bicycle down beside the railroad tracks and was ready to launch one of the stones from the railroad bed.

"Wait a minute," he shouted.

But it was too late; Eep had already thrown the first of his handful of rocks. Before he could say another word, the rest of the boys were firing rocks at the huge hornet nest.

"Wait a minute," Moe shouted again.

Finally one of the rocks tore into the side of the nest leaving a small hole where several of the large flying creatures began to exit.

"That was a lucky shot," said Eep.

"No. it wasn't," said Wart. "I only threw one rock and I can hit it again."

"Betcha can't."

Now all the boys gathered around as the oldest and youngest members of their group started laying out the ground rules for the bet.

"Okay, I'll bet you I can hit that hornets' nest before you can," said Wart.

"Okay, but what's the bet?"

"If you hit it first, I'll buy your candy at the movie next week."

"Okay, you've got a deal," said Eep.

"But if I hit it first, then you have to buy my candy," said Wart.

"Okay, but I'm the smallest. I get to go first."

Eep was in fact the youngest of the group, but even though he was older Wart was an inch shorter than Eep. What he lacked in size, Wart more than made up for in determination. The whole group knew he was the fastest, most athletic of all the River Rats.

"All right, take your best shot," said Wart. "You're only going to get one."

The hornets' nest hung from the rock cliff almost a hundred feet above the boys. Eep looked around for the perfect rock, finally finding one that seemed to feel just right in his hand.

"We'll throw until one of us hits the hornets' nest," said Eep.

"Read my lips--I only need one rock," said Wart.

"You're so full of baloney," said Eep.

"If that's what you think, then how about we up the bet."

"To what?"

"The loser pays the other's way into the movie as well as buying his candy."

"Eep, don't do it," said his brother. "If you lose, you won't have enough money to get into the movie."

"I'm not going to lose."

"Then fire away," said Wart.

Eep stared intently at the hornets' nest. He knew that the rest of the guys would make fun of him for a long time if he missed. He looked at his brother and then at the rest of the River Rats. He knew he had made a terrible mistake in challenging Wart. Wart didn't back down from anything, which was usually a plus for the group, but had on occasion gotten them into trouble.

"Maybe we could just go back to the candy bet," Eep finally said.

"If that's what you want, then candy it is," said Wart. "You wanted to throw first, so give it your best shot."

Eep again stared at the nest, but his stomach felt a little better since being able to get into the movie was no longer on the line. He finally took a deep breath and let the rock fly.

It hit just to the right of the nest and fell away harmlessly.

"I'd like the biggest bag of M&M Peanut candy," said Wart.

"You've got to hit the nest first," said Eep.

Wart reached down, picked up a rock the size of a golf ball and let it fly. The rock tore into the side of the big nest, ripping a hole the size of one of Wart's hands. The boys stood frozen for a moment until they realized that the hornets were pouring out of the nest and they weren't the least bit happy.

Unfortunately, Dill had already heaved another rock in the direction of the nest. The hornets looked like a large black mass moving around the nest until Dill's rock sailed by. This gave the hornets a direction to head towards and the giant black flying mass started towards the River Rats with stingers fully loaded.

Tooth, Tank and Beau had seen the hornets gathering before Dill had thrown his rock. They had jumped on their bikes and taken off down the tracks right away. Wart, realizing what he had started, took off behind them.

"Let's get out of here," yelled Moe, as he followed Wart.

Dill and Eep were left staring upwards at the giant flying mass of angry hornets just as they began diving in their direction. Dill left his bike and took off running away from the hornets. He was much faster than Eep and quickly caught up with Moe. Looking back at the dark cloud of hornets moving towards them, the boys realized that they wouldn't get far before the angry insects caught them and Eep was definitely going to feel the wrath of those stingers.

"When you get to the railroad bridge," yelled Moe. "Jump."

The boys had walked these tracks for years and knew every inch of the railroad tracks, the bridges, the tunnels and the creeks. They had jumped off this bridge on several occasions, so jumping the fifteen feet to the water below was no big deal and this time it might mean the difference between getting stung or not.

Tooth, Tank and Beau reached the bridge first and left their bicycles on the side of the tracks. Racing out onto the bridge, they jumped when they reached the halfway point without stopping to look back.

Wart reached the bridge next and looking back over his shoulder, he could see Dill was about to pass Moe. Eep stayed barely in front of the large mass of insects bearing down on him.

Wart dropped his bike and jumped over the side of the bridge, followed closely by Dill. Moe kept yelling at his brother to hurry up. Moe waited until Eep reached the edge of the bridge before he finally jumped over the side.

The first hornet hit Eep on the back of his left arm just above the elbow. The second caught him in the middle of his back. The third sting caught him on the left shoulder just as he jumped off the bridge.

The hornets didn't follow the boys down to the creek below the bridge, so with no one left to sting, the angry hornets hovered a minute and then began flying back towards their nest.

Fifteen minutes later Moe looked around and said, "I think we can go back and get our bikes."

"What about mine?" asked Eep.

"Good question. What about yours?" asked his brother.

"Aren't you going to go back and get it for me?"

"You left it. You go back and get it."

"I'll tell Mom."

"And I'll tell her the whole story," said Moe.

"Will you walk back with me?" asked Eep.

"I will," said Dill. "My bike is back there, but if you make one sound or pick up one rock you're dog meat."

"I'll tell my Mom."

"And I don't care."

"Okay," said Eep, meekly.

The two boys walked back very slowly and very quietly to where they had left their bikes. The hornets were already busy rebuilding their giant nest. Dill and Eep picked up their bikes and just as slowly and quietly began to push them back in the direction of the railroad bridge they had jumped from. The rest of the boys waited on the far side of the bridge.

"How long are we going to ride down these tracks?" asked Beau.

"Just down to the golf course," said Wart. "Then we cut across Route 2 and head out Bull Ridge Road.

The fog had lifted completely as the boys rode their bikes out Bull Ridge. Reaching the first big hill, Beau quit pedaling and started pushing his bike before he got halfway up. Only Wart rode his bike all the way to the top.

When they had all finally reached the top, Moe said, "Beau, you have to be careful going down this side. There are a couple of big turns and if you get going too fast you might not stop even if you hit your brakes. The dirt and gravel won't stop you from going over the hill and it's a long drop to the creek below."

"Why don't you follow me?" said Tooth. "I don't go as fast down this hill as some of these idiots."

"Do you guys come out here often?" asked Beau.

"Two or three times a summer," said Tooth. "But we're not going all the way today. Dill just said that last night, so the girls wouldn't want to come along. We'll cut back across to the cemetery and then down off Gas Line Hill."

"Its only about five miles total," said Tank. "Then we'll stop at Dead-Man's Leap."

Beau shuddered at the mention of the place. "Did anyone ever really die there?"

"That's a good question," said Wart. "Does anybody know?"

They all shook their heads.

"It looks like someone would've died if they jumped off there," said Moe. "I guess we kind of gave it its name."

Beau gave a sigh of relief. Maybe it wouldn't be so bad after all, he thought.

They made it down off Bull Ridge and an hour later Dead-Man's Leap came into sight.

"Here we are. That's Dead-Man's Leap up there," said Moe, pointing at an outcropping about two hundred feet straight up the cliff in front of them.

"Are you nuts? There's no way I'm going to jump off that thing," said Beau. "Beside, how would you ever get up there in the first place?"

"Well, we have to leave out bikes here and hike on foot up that trail over there," Moe said.

Beau could see Wart and Tooth already starting up a path between two large pine trees.

"Well, I'm not going," said Beau.

"Are you chicken?" asked Eep.

"I'm not chicken and I'm not stupid," said Beau.

"Well, if I can jump off and you're afraid, then

you're chicken." Eep took off up the path behind his brother.

"Listen, just come along with us. If you don't want to jump, then you don't have to," said Dill. "I'll walk back down with you whenever you want to."

Beau nodded and started climbing up the path. The first hundred feet were close to straight up, but after that it wound back and forth until they finally reached the top.

"Wait a minute," said Beau. "That rock doesn't face out over the cliff."

"We know," said Wart.

"But from down there it looks like if you jump off that rock, you're going to land on the road where we were standing."

"That's right."

"How did you guys find this place?" he asked.

"My older brother," said Tank. "He and his friends found it a long time ago."

"We've been coming up every summer for as long as we could climb," said Wart.

"It still looks pretty high to jump off of," said Beau.

"Look," said Eep, who had already climbed to the top of the rock.

He spread out his arms and jumped feet first off the rock face away from the rest of the boys.

"Where did he go?" shouted Beau.

"Right here," said Eep, coming around the face of the big rock outcropping.

"I don't understand," said Beau.

The boys climbed to the top of the rock and looked over the edge. Below, Beau could see that the hillside slanted away from the base of the rock at about a forty-five-degree angle.

"It's still a long way down there," said Beau. "It must be at least ten feet."

"Yeah, but if you land on your feet and fall back on your butt, the shale rock will give you a soft landing," said Wart. "Watch."

Wart walked to the edge of the rock and jumped out away from it. His feet hit the ground first and then he leaned back against the hillside and slid with the rocks.

"That's amazing," said Beau. "Can I try it?"

"Sure, but wait a minute until Tank jumps," said Moe. "We always have at least two guys waiting to catch first-timers, in case they land wrong."

Beau's turn finally came and as he walked to the edge of the rock, his stomach began inching up into his throat. He could see out to the Ohio River in the distance and the town of Monley a little to the north. What a beautiful sight, he thought.

"Are you going to jump or what?" hollered Tank.

Beau moved forward, spread out his arms like he had seen Eep do, bent his knees and jumped forward feet first. As he sailed through the air, Beau could feel the wind rush past his face and even though the feeling only lasted a moment, he knew what it must feel like to fly.

Hitting the ground, he leaned back and slid in the shale rock for about fifteen feet before Tank grabbed his arm and pulled him up.

"Wow, what a feeling. I've got to do that again," he cried.

The boys took turns jumping off the cliff until they were all so tired from climbing that they just sat on Dead-Man's Leap and looked out over the valley below.

"You know, Uncle Jim was right," said Beau. "This is a beautiful place. I see why he loves it here."

"Well, guys, what do you think?" asked Moe. "Is Beau a River Rat?"

Every head nodded in agreement as they laughed.

"There's one more thing," said Moe. "You can't tell anyone where this place is. It's ours and no one else's."

"I swear," said Beau. "I have got to come back here someday."

The boys spent the next hour resting, eating lunch and admiring the view before heading back down to where they had left their bikes.

Looking up at Dead-Man's Leap, Beau said, "I wish I had a picture of this. The guys back home will never believe that I climbed up there, let alone jumped off."

"What do you say we celebrate at the Dairy Queen on the way home?" said Wart.

"I could use a Mr. Misty," said Tank.

"Sure," said Moe. "Let's celebrate Beau joining the River Rats."

The boys hopped on their bikes and headed back towards town. Having a downhill ride all the way back, the boys weaved back and forth down the crooked road. Each tried to outperform the others with feats of bikemanship on the way. Dill and Beau rode at the back of the pack, taking it all in.

"Sometimes I think they're nuts," Dill confessed to Beau.

"Yeah, I know what you mean," said Beau, pointing at Wart who was riding with his feet up on the handlebars.

Finally arriving at the Dairy Queen, Beau said, "I never would have believed there was a Dairy Queen in this town. I'm amazed."

"Monley may be small, but we've got it all--or at least that's what the mayor says," said Wart.

The boys all laughed as Eep stepped up to the counter.

"I'll have a grape Mr. Misty," he said.

Each of the boys ordered one of the icy Dairy Queen treats in various flavors.

Eep walked away from the counter and immediately began to suck on the straw drawing the ice-cold drink into his mouth. It tasted like the nectar of the gods. Finally, after finishing over half the container's contents, Eep turned loose the straw, taking an unsteady step backwards.

Tooth looked at Dill as both began to laugh. "Brain freeze," they said together.

Eep's face had contorted and his eyes were closed as he bent forward to steady himself.

"Wow," he said. "That was good."

All the River Rats laughed as Eep shook his head trying to clear away the freezing sensation in his face that had come from swallowing so much of the icy treat so fast.

Chapter Nineteen

❧—The midway had filled up with people long before the boys got there that afternoon. Along with Lucy, Alexis and Deanie, the boys wandered up and down the rows of games watching as people tried their luck at different tests of skills.

The afternoon circus performance had just ended, but before the crowd could exit the big top, a storm came rushing over the hills from Ohio. It first appeared as black clouds coming from the west, but within minutes the wind picked up and began to blow around anything not tied down. Finally the rain came. Sheets of it were coming at them almost sideways. For a while, hail the size of grapes fell all over Monley, but that stopped before any real damage was done.

The carnival and circus workers had seen the

storm coming and immediately had begun tying everything down securely. The rides were all stopped and locked in place. The rest of the open-air booths took their prizes down and stored them inside while they rode out the wind and rain.

"Oh, man, this is terrible. We've only got today and tomorrow left until the circus and carnival leaves and it looks like today is shot," Dill said, looking out from the big top where they had run to take cover.

"Maybe it will pass. Maybe they'll open the midway later. Maybe..."

"Maybe you'll get a brain, but I doubt that too," Dill said to Tooth, cutting him off.

The rain continued to pour down.

The storm had come up so suddenly and the wind was so strong that two-foot white caps began appearing on the Ohio River within minutes after the storm had crossed the hills west of Monley.

The ferryboat, Big Moses, had never been in any

real danger, but it had been tossed around a bit on one of its trips. Just as it left the West Virginia shore, a particularly large wave crashed over the front of the boat, splashing all the cars and jerking the boat sideways. Everyone on the ferry was okay, but one silent passenger no longer accompanied the others. A dark form slid from under the car carrier and slipped unnoticed back towards the West Virginia shore. Driven by the wind and waves, it floated just inches under the surface of the dark water.

All the Marine Patrol search boats had headed for shore when the waves began appearing, so the ghostly figure in the water again evaded detection as it floated just off shore from hundreds of people who were now fleeing the wind and rain of the rising storm.

Chief Todd scanned the river, looking for any clue as to what was going on in his town, but saw nothing. Finally, wet and wind blown he turned his back to the water and began walking towards his squad car. As he did, the body broke the surface of the water as if to taunt the police officer. Unfortunately he had already turned away and was wiping the water from his glasses.

Chief Todd felt that something strange was happening in Monley, but as yet couldn't put his finger on what it was. He had one of those feelings in his gut that just didn't sit right.

Reaching the squad car, he looked down at his mud-covered boots. He hated dragging all that mud and water into his brand new Chevy Impala. First those boys had stunk up his new car and now all this mud. The town had finally broken down and bought a new cruiser and he was determined to keep it in as good shape as possible, for as long as possible. The old cruiser had been a second-hand model from the Wheeling Police Department. It had lasted six years, which was a lot longer than anyone expected.

Sliding in under the steering wheel, he could

feel the old pain in his knee reappearing. It always started that way when it got wet or cold. Right now he didn't have time for the inconvenience of a bum leg. He was on the scent of something that would drive him until he found the answers he knew were out there. He just couldn't see them yet.

He started the Chevy, listening for a minute to its throaty roar. He knew that if he needed it, this car could run with the best of them. The town hadn't skimped on this one. Someday all that power would come in handy, but today he needed to do a little research. The State Police might have some information that could help.

Chapter Twenty

❧ For the next fifteen minutes, the wind continued to blow and the rain poured down. Then just as suddenly as it began, it ended.

"Hey, look. There's a rainbow. I told you it might stop," Tooth said.

"Even a blind squirrel finds an acorn now and then," said Dill.

"What? What does that mean?" asked Eep.

"Everybody gets lucky once in a while is what it means."

The scream came from the lady standing all alone a hundred yards south of where the Marine Patrol boats had tied up during the storm. Her shriek drowned out all the commotion at the ferryboat landing. Everyone turned at once to see the young woman just as she fell face down on the riverbank.

Her head lay half submerged in the water, while the rest of her body lay motionless.

The stunned crowd stood frozen stiff until Chief Todd screamed, "Help her. Somebody help her."

The entire crowd moved at once, but two men who were closest reached her first and pulled her out of the water. She began coughing and sputtering. Her face was covered with the slimy sand of the riverbank. Her once clean white blouse now had dark mud stains all over it.

Chief Todd pushed his way through the crowd. "Excuse me. Let me through. Will you all step back and let me through?"

Finally the crowd made a pathway for the Chief.

"Call the rescue unit. I want an ambulance down here now."

"Who is she? Does anyone know who she is?" he continued.

"I don't know," said the man kneeling beside her.

"Miss! Can you hear me? Miss! What is your name?" the Chief asked.

The young woman raised her head and said, "What happened?"

"We thought you might tell us. First, what is your name?"

"Name. Oh yeah, my name is Sharon Welks."

"What happened, Sharon? Can you tell us what happened?"

"Yes," she said slowly. "I saw something in the water. When I walked down the bank a face came up out of the water and said, 'Follow me.'"

"Follow me," said Chief Todd. "Are you sure that's what it said?"

"Yes, sir. It was as plain as anything I've ever heard. But, it came up out of the water."

"What happened then?"

"I don't remember anything until you started

asking me questions," Sharon Welks said. "I don't remember anything else at all."

"Where are you from, Sharon?" asked the Chief. "Are you here with anyone?"

"Yes. I'm here with my boyfriend. He went to ride on the roller coaster. I don't like those things, so I came over the river bank to watch the boats."

"What's your boyfriend's name, Sharon?"

"Andy. Andy Holcomb. We're from up in Haverville. We came down for the carnival. I wish we had stayed home."

The Chief pointed to two men he knew in the crowd and instructed them to go to the roller coaster and find Andy Holcomb. "Use the carnival's PA system if necessary," he said. "But find him and bring him back here."

He turned back to the young woman. "It's going to be okay. You're going to be all right. We've got an ambulance coming and they'll take you to the hospital."

"I'm okay. Really. I'm okay," she said. "If you'll help me up, I think I'll be all right."

As she started to stand, her knees buckled under her. The two men who had pulled her out of the water again grabbed hold of her and gently helped her sit back down.

"I think it would be a good idea if you waited here until the ambulance comes. The doctors can check you out at the hospital and if you're okay, then you can go on home," said Chief Todd.

A tall young man burst through the crowd and knelt beside the young woman.

"Sharon, are you all right?" he asked.

"Yes, I think I am, but the policeman wants me to go to the hospital."

"I think it would be a good idea if they checked her out, before she goes home. She's got a nasty bump on her forehead and something has frightened her very badly," said the Chief.

"Sure. Whatever you say," said the young man.

"Whatever you say is fine. Thank you. Thank all of you."

Wrapping his arms around the young woman, he sat on the riverbank with her waiting for the ambulance.

Motioning to one of the men standing in the crowd, Chief Todd instructed him to find the head of the Marine Patrol and bring him there immediately. The Chief then told several of the men present to investigate the area along the riverbank where the woman had fallen. They were to scan the water for anything unusual and yell out for help if they spotted anything.

When the Marine Patrol Captain arrived, the Chief told him what had happened and where. He wanted the search moved to that area along the riverbank. If they hurried, they might be able to find what was in the water.

Sharon Welks' description matched what Maye Vern had seen. A ghostly face appears from under the muddy waters of the Ohio River and says, "Follow me." Chief Todd kept trying to put the pieces together, but he knew that something was missing. But what? The dots just didn't connect. There had to be some missing piece to this puzzle.

A few minutes later Wart came running up to the group just as they were leaving the tent. The others started asking him questions about where he had been during the storm. He kept getting interrupted before he could answer.

"Will you guys shut up?" Wart said. "I just heard that the ghost reappeared a few minutes ago."

"Where?" asked Moe. "Where did it show up this time?"

"Just below the ferry landing."

"That's only a few hundred yards from here. Let's go."

"What about the midway?" asked Eep.

"You go to the midway," said Moe. "We're headed for the river."

Chapter Twenty-One

•&—"Should we go home and get our bathing suits?"

"No, Eep, we don't need bathing suits," said Moe. "We're going down to the river to see if we can find out what happened."

The boys started walking down the midway, taking in all the sights and sounds on the way to the river.

"I'm hungry," said Eep.

"You had popcorn, ice cream, a hot dog and cotton candy. Have you got a hollow leg?" asked Moe.

"No."

"I think he has a hollow head," said Wart.

"What do you think happened with the body?" asked Alexis.

"I don't know," said Wart. "All I heard was that it had shown up again. I don't think anyone really knows what's going on."

"I know," said a voice from behind them. "It's a Mountain Man."

"Baloney, Al. You've been trying to scare people with that story for years," said Tank.

"Nobody's ever seen one of those Mountain Men," said Tooth.

"That's not true," Al Dristen answered. "About five years ago, someone saw one of them over in Ritchie County. The year before that someone saw one in Tyler County."

"Who saw them? Give me a name and I'll call them," said Eep.

"It's not a club. We don't get in touch with each other, but some people over at West Virginia University were interested enough to come over and investigate."

"Really," said Tooth.

"Yeah. Really."

"But why would a Mountain Man or Big Foot or Sasquatch or whatever it's called be swimming in the river and scaring people?" asked Tooth.

"That's the mystery," said Al. "Now, isn't it."

Al turned and walked in the opposite direction that the River Rats were headed.

"He's a strange old coot," said Deanie.

"Yes, he is," said Dill. "But he's also a smart old coot. He graduated from WVU and Ohio State. He's a member in a whole bunch of special clubs and groups that do research."

"He sounds smart," said Deanie.

"He's nuts," said Tooth. "Don't you think he's nuts?"

"Well, uh--I don't know," answered Dill.

"Listen, I know you think he's smart, but you can be smart and nuts at the same time."

"Well, he definitely is smart and I'll agree he's a little squirrelly, but I don't think he's a certifiable nut job."

"Come on, you guys," said Moe. "Time's wasting. Somebody else will have found out what this is all about and we won't even be there."

Moe picked up the pace until the whole group was moving at a gallop towards the river.

Chapter Twenty-Two

❖—After all the commotion had finally settled down, the River Rats began walking towards home.

"I think we can find the body," said Moe.

"I think you all are crazy," said Beau. "The police and Marine Patrol haven't found it yet, so what makes you think we can find it."

A silence fell over the group as they all thought about what Beau had said.

Finally, Eep broke the silence. "We could borrow a boat and row up and down the shore," he said.

Wart laughed. "That's a pretty dumb idea."

"Why is it a dumb idea?" asked Eep.

"Well, just because."

"Maybe that isn't a completely dumb idea," said

Moe. "We are probably going to need a boat. Why don't we ask Jim Hampton if we can borrow his yacht?"

The boys all laughed at the thought of Jim's "yacht." It was in fact a ten-foot aluminum johnboat that he used for fishing. Jim called it his yacht and from time to time he would let the boys borrow it.

"How about if we camp out next to the river? That way we will be sure to see the body or whatever it is if it comes up again," said Wart.

"Hey, that's a great idea," said Tooth. "We can get our scout tents and--"

"No," said Moe. "We can't do anything where people, especially Chief Todd, will know what we are doing. Besides, our parents would go berserk if we got in trouble with the law again."

"Right. You guys remember last summer when we found those bones?" said Dill.

"Yeah. And we all ended up in jail," said

Tooth.

"Jail. Bones. Bodies. What goes on in this town?" asked Beau.

"Listen. We didn't get into any real trouble and it's a long story. I'll tell you later, but we are going to need your help," said Moe. "Will you help us?"

"Come on. You're a River Rat. You can't back out," Tank said.

"Yeah, you're one of us," said Eep.

"All right. All right. But what are we going to do?"

"Well, we've got to be a little smarter than the average bear," said Tank. "I think we can cover everything from seven-thirty this evening until midnight. If the body comes up later than that, we probably won't see it anyway."

"Tank's got a great idea. We can patrol the river bank from the ferryboat south," said Moe. "It's for sure it isn't going up stream. Two of us can set up a lookout post at the south end of town," said Moe.

"How about if Tooth and I set up watch at the south end of Fullcross Island?" asked Dill.

The two boys looked at each other smiling. Tooth punched Dill in the arm and nodded in complete agreement.

"Okay," said Moe. "If either of you spots anything, the other one comes and gets the rest of us. Is that agreed?"

"Sure," said both boys.

"Now, what else can we do?"

"How about if we patrol the shore in twos? You know, back and forth," said Tank. "That way we will be able to cover more ground and always have someone to run for help."

"Sounds like a plan," said Moe. "We'll put Jim's boat at the mouth of Clear Creek. That's halfway between the ferryboat landing and where Tooth and Dill will be. That way we can pick it up and move it either way when we need it. Anything else?"

"Yeah. Who gets stuck with Eep?" asked Tank.

"I'll take him with me," said Moe. "Anything else?"

"What do you mean, stuck?" Eep asked. "I can do anything you guys can do and probably a lot more."

"Yeah, right," said Tank.

"Listen, lay off of him," said Moe. "I'm warning you. Just leave him alone."

"When do we start and who is going to ask Jim about the boat?" asked Wart.

"Why don't you ask him on your way home and we can get started right after supper. Is that okay?"

"What about going to the carnival this evening?" asked Eep.

"If you want to go to the carnival, then you can go by yourself. It will still be here tomorrow, but I really think if we go down to the river this evening we can find whatever is out there."

With all questions answered, the boys started home for dinner agreeing to meet back at Moe's house at seven o'clock.

Chapter Twenty-Three

❧ On the dot of seven, Tooth, Dill, Tank and Wart stood on Moe's back porch. Beau showed up a few minutes later. Mrs. Pitman saw them through the kitchen window and walked toward the back door to let them in.

"It's okay, Mom--we're going to head downtown for awhile. Come on, Eep, the guys are ready to go."

Eep scooped a last bite of mashed potatoes and gravy into his mouth before jumping up to join his brother.

"Whoa. Didn't you forget something?" their father said, in a very stern voice.

"Sorry," replied Eep, as he grabbed his knife, fork, plate and empty milk glass.

"That's better."

"What time are you going to be back?" asked Mrs. Pitman.

"Can we stay out a little later tonight, Mom?" asked Moe. "The carnival's in town and..." he continued, letting his voice trail off to a murmur.

"Okay, what time are you thinking?" she asked.

"I think the carnival is open until midnight. Would that be okay?"

"You be sure to keep Eep with you all the time."

"Yes, ma'am, I will."

"Are you all going together?"

"Yes, ma'am."

"Okay. Have a good time and be quiet when you come in."

As the group walked down the alley behind Moe's house, he asked, "Can everyone stay out until midnight?"

All heads nodded in agreement.

"Wart, did you get Jim's boat?" Moe asked.

"Couldn't."

"Why? What's the deal?"

"He's going fishing with my dad early tomorrow morning," said Beau "I'm sorry."

"What was I supposed to do?" said Wart.

"Nothing, I guess. We'll just have to figure something else out."

"Hey, wait a minute. Why don't we get those ropes that we had for Boy Scout camp last spring?" said Tooth.

"That's a great idea, but Eep and I can't go back home looking for ropes. My mom will get suspicious. She'll know something's up."

"Tooth and I have three at home. We kept that extra one we made," said Dill. "How many do we need anyway?"

"Well, there are going to be three groups and I guess we only need one rope each, so that should be enough," said Moe. "Why don't you guys get your ropes and meet us at the ferry landing."

As they walked down the alley, they heard Jim Hampton's booming voice. "Do you boys still want the yacht?"

Wart ran over to the Hampton's back door, followed by Tank, Moe and Eep. "Yes, sir. Aren't you going to need it?" he asked.

"No, I won't be needing it tomorrow, but I want it back by tomorrow evening, okay?"

"That's perfect," said Moe. "Could we go ahead and take it tonight?"

"Why do you want it tonight?" Jim asked.

"Well," Moe stammered, "We don't want to wake anyone up when we leave in the morning."

"That's really considerate of you boys. I'm sure Mrs. Hampton will appreciate that. I know Lucy will too."

"I'd like to wake her up," mumbled Eep.

"What was that, Eep?" asked the big man.

"He says thanks," said Moe. "And so do the rest

of us. We'll have it back tomorrow afternoon."

"Okay. You boys have a good time and good luck."

Grabbing the aluminum boat, the boys literally flew down the alley. Luckily Jim Hampton didn't notice that his boat wasn't staying in the neighborhood that night. If he had seen it turn the corner at the end of the alley, he would have wondered what the boys were up to. But their luck held and once again they headed for the ferryboat landing.

When they reached the landing, Tooth and Dill were already there.

"How did you get the boat?" they asked in unison.

"Jim just came out and gave it to us," said Eep, smiling.

"Why?"

"He said he wasn't going to need it and all we had to do was get it back to him by tomorrow evening," Wart replied.

"Okay, now what do we do?" asked Dill.

"Let's go with the original plan. We'll tie the boat up to the big tree at the mouth of Clear Creek. Anyone who spots something sends the other one for the rest of us. That way we can get the boat and use it to get out on the river. We'll each have a rope and if the thing comes close to shore, lasso it and hang on until the rest of us can get there," Moe explained. "Any questions?"

"What if someone sees us and asks what we're doing?" asked Dill.

"Tell them you're looking for night crawlers. Tell them you're going fishing in the morning and you're looking for bait," said Tank.

"That should do it," said Moe. "Anything else? Okay, we'll patrol back and forth. Dill, you and Tooth will need to have one of you always at the end of Fullcross Island. You can switch off patrolling up to the sewage treatment plant. Eep and I will take from the sewage plant to Clear Creek. Tank and Beau will patrol from the creek to the ferryboat landing."

"Hey, what about me?" asked Wart.

"Since you're the fastest, why don't you just wander back and forth between groups? That way you're probably going to be close when something happens," said Moe.

"Okay, sounds good."

With that, the boys set off to their appointed sites. A few minutes after reaching the end of Fullcross Island, Tooth and Dill were approached by a couple of boys they knew from school.

"What are you guys doing out here?" the bigger of the two asked. "I figured everyone was at the carnival."

"Nah, we're hunting night crawlers," said Dill.

"Really," the small boy with the flat-top haircut said.

"Where's your can?" asked the bigger boy.

"Didn't you bring the can, Dill?" asked Tooth

"No, I thought you did," Dill replied.

"Boy, are you two stupid," commented flat-top.

"You know what I think?" asked the bigger boy. "I think you're out here looking for that body. That's what I think."

"What body?" asked Dill.

"You guys really are stupid, aren't you?" said flat-top.

The two intruders walked off laughing, but before they got too far they picked up a couple of dirt clods that were lying along the riverbank. The first one whistled past Dill's left ear. The second one caught Tooth square in the chest.

The two River Rats picked up dirt clods in each hand and started to chase the intruders. Tooth grabbed Dill's arm and pulled him to a stop.

"Listen, we can get those guys any time, but Moe and the guys are going to be mad if we don't stay out here and look for that body," he said.

"Yeah, I know. You're right, but when this is all over, we are going to get them back. Right?"

"Oh yeah. You can count on it."

"Look. What is that?" Dill was pointing towards the end of Fullcross Island.

"I don't know. It could be the body," said Tooth. "It sure is something."

"Do you think we should get the rest of the guys?"

"No. I'll wade out and see if I can pull it in."

"Do you want me to go with you?"

"Why don't you hold on to this end of the rope? I'll tie it onto whatever that is and you can help pull it back in. If it's something important, you can run for the rest of the guys."

"Good idea."

The sun hadn't gone down behind the Ohio side hills yet, so as Tooth waded into the murky water he could still see clearly. The object kept bobbing, just barely breaking the river's surface.

As Tooth got close, the depth of the water had risen to his armpits and he began to swim. The object floated only a hundred feet away and Tooth knew the current would bring it to where he stood.

Treading water and waiting for the object seemed to take forever. Finally as the sun sunk below the western hills, it surfaced again. Tooth took off swimming as fast as he could towards the unknown object.

As he reached it, it began to submerge again. Reaching out, he grabbed for the mysterious thing.

"Did you get it?" Dill yelled from on shore.

Tooth didn't answer right away as he tried to hold on to the object.

"What is it? Can you tell what it is?" Dill shouted, now waist deep in the water.

Finally Tooth turned and began to swim back

•—171—•

towards shore.

Reaching a spot where he could stand up, he looked at his brother and said, "It was a tree limb. The end of it looked like a head until you got really close to it. I could feel the branches on it just under the water. There were still leaves on the thing," Tooth explained.

"Man. I thought we had it."

"Yeah, me too."

"Oh well, we tried."

As the Simmons brothers began patrolling their area again, Moe began to wonder why he hadn't seen Dill or Tooth at the meeting point of their areas. Just then Wart came strolling up from the opposite direction.

"Listen, Wart, we haven't seen Dill or Tooth for a while. Why don't you run down and see what's happening--"

Moe got cut off in mid sentence as Dill came out of a stand of rhododendron bushes.

"Hey. We thought we saw something, so Tooth swam out to check it out."

"Well. What was it?" asked Eep.

"A branch. Tooth is resting right now. I'm going to take the next couple of turns up and back. How about you guys?"

"We saw a dog, but General Jackson swam out and chased it away," said Eep.

"Where is the General?" asked Dill.

"I don't know. He's off looking for a bone or a girlfriend, I guess," said Moe.

All four boys laughed. They all knew that the General had a reputation of being a ladies' man.

Chapter Twenty-Four

The next couple of hours passed with nothing happening until Tooth heard the General's excited barking in the distance.

"I'll check it out," he said.

"Fine. I'm getting tired. I'll stay here and look out for the boogey-man or whatever is out there," said Dill.

Tooth walked along the river's shoreline like he had a thousand other times. The trees looked the same. The old rotted out stumps looked the same. Even the old abandoned rotting rowboat, with the number sixteen still visible, looked the same, but the thing the General continued to bark at hadn't been there fifteen minutes ago.

"Dill. Dill," Tooth shouted at the top of his lungs. "Come quick. There's something up here."

About fifty feet out from the shore, a round object, about the size of a large melon appeared to be trapped by a broken tree branch hanging down in the water, but with one end still attached to the trunk of a tree somewhere above Tooth's head.

In the pale moonlight two shiny red eyes were staring at Tooth. He felt the hair on his neck begin to tingle while a sickening feeling ran through his stomach. He heard a gurgling sound coming from whatever was in the river.

At this point he could no longer yell. His voice kept getting stuck somewhere between his non-existent tonsils and that large lump in his throat. Only a barely audible creaking sound came out of Tooth.

The General kept barking and darting back and forth along the water's edge. Even he knew that something wasn't right about that thing in the water. Normally the General didn't need an excuse to jump in the river, but tonight he wasn't going in the water. He stayed at the edge growling and barking.

Tooth stood motionless, staring at the red eyes in the distance, when from the direction of the red eyes he heard, "Follow me. I'll show you the way."

With that, Tooth turned and ran toward his brother. The creaking sound he kept making got louder the farther he ran. By the time he reached Dill, he was screaming at the top of his lungs, "I've seen the Devil. I've seen the Devil and he wants me to follow him."

"Whoa. What are you talking about?"

"I've seen the Devil and he has red eyes and he wanted me to follow him."

"No. No. That ain't happening. Don't even say that," said Dill.

"Do you hear that dog barking? He's barking at the Devil and I'm getting out of here."

"Listen to me," said Dill.

"No. I know what you're going to say and I'm not going back up there," said Tooth.

"Okay. Okay. Tell me exactly what you saw. I'll keep an eye on it and you go get the rest of the guys."

"No. Don't go out there. I swear I've never seen anything like that. I think Mrs. Wheatly was right. It's a ghost or the Devil. I know it's something bad. Please, Dill, don't go out there."

"I'm going. If you'd tell me what I'm looking for, it would help a lot."

"All right. Jeez-uie, I don't like doing this. I'll go back with you and then I'll get the rest of the guys."

The two brothers crept slowly and as quietly as possible towards the sound of the dog's barking. They could see the General at the water's edge, just past a large stand of reeds. The dog's lips were pulled back exposing his teeth as he growled a low menacing sound that the boys had never heard from him before.

"There. There it is," said Tooth. "See those red eyes. It talked to me a minute ago. Please don't go out there."

"Go get the rest of the guys and hurry," said Dill.

Tooth took off running towards where he knew Moe and Eep would be patrolling.

Dill took a deep breath and walked over to the General.

"It's okay, boy," he said. "Let's see what this thing is."

The dog stopped barking, but continued the low guttural growl as Dill waded into the water.

"Follow me. I'll show you the way," came a voice from the river.

"Holy moly," shouted Dill, as his stomach tried to come up through his throat. The hair on the back of his neck stood up and a tingle ran down his spine. He could barely make his legs move, but here he stood in knee-deep water. He knew he had to do something. Turn around and run or try to find out what this thing in the river was.

"I'm coming," he said. "I'm going to follow you."

He thought if he talked to it, maybe it would tell him who it was.

"Where are you? Where did you go?"

The river was still. Only the General's low growls broke the silence.

"What are--"

The red eyes appeared again, but now they were less than twenty feet from him. This time Dill didn't feel quite so brave. He began to backtrack towards shore when he heard the rest of the River Rats come plowing through the reeds along the riverbank.

"I'm out here. It's out here. Bring the boat."

The General kept barking as the boat hit the water. Moe and Tank jumped in and began paddling towards Dill.

"We're coming," yelled Eep.

Wart and Tooth ran straight into the water and quickly reached Dill's side.

"Where is it?" asked Tank.

"I don't know. It was here a minute ago. It was about twenty feet out in that direction," said Dill, pointing straight out into the river.

Moe looked at Tank and said, "Take the boat about fifty feet down stream. Tooth, get in the boat with Tank."

With that, Moe jumped out of the boat and Tooth crawled in.

"Eep, have you got the rope?" Moe asked.

"Yeah. Do you want me to lasso it?"

"No. Give it to Tank and Tooth."

"I get it," said Tank. "You want us to be down stream and you guys are going to chase it down to us."

"Exactly. And when it gets close, lasso it," said

Moe.

"Hey, I wanted to lasso it," said Eep.

"Next time, little brother."

"That's not fair," said Eep.

"Tonight isn't about being fair. We're trying to catch this thing and Tank and Tooth are a lot bigger and stronger than you," said his brother.

Actually Moe didn't want his brother to be in a position to get hurt. He knew that if anything happened to Eep, he would have to pay the consequences.

"I think if the five of us wade out just a few feet apart, then we should be able to see it if it reappears. If we don't get it tonight, it will be past the last island for thirty miles and who knows if anyone will ever find out what this thing is," said Moe.

"Okay," said Wart. "I'm going to go first. Do you want to go next, Beau?"

"Sure, what the heck. I feel like wrestling with a ghost tonight."

"Okay. I'll go next," said Moe.

"What about me?" asked Eep.

"You've got to stay with the General. He's the one who can spot this thing," said Moe. "You're the scout. You and the General keep an eye on the water and let us know if you see anything."

"I guess I'll go last," said Dill.

Wart walked out until the water reached his shoulders. "I'm going to have to swim from here on," he said.

"I saw it just a little bit down stream from where you are now," said Dill.

"We're ready," said Tank.

"Everybody be quiet and keep watching the water," said Moe.

The fog had started drifting in off the river shortly after the boys had started their hunt. The wispy light gray sheets of fog didn't impair their ability to see, but they did lend an air of mystery and foreboding to the night.

"Do you guys see anything?" shouted Tank.

"No, how about you?" Moe answered.

"No. Nothing. Where do you think it went?"

"I don't know, but it can't have gotten far."

The boys kept wading with the current, but no one could see a thing. Even the General had stopped barking. He kept peering out towards the river, but made no attempt to enter the water.

"Look."

At the same time that Wart shouted, the General began barking and growling and hopping all over the place next to Eep.

"Where?" screamed Tooth.

"There. Right beside the boat," yelled Wart.

Tooth looked over the side of the boat and saw a pair of red eyes looking straight up at him. The face floated just below the surface of the water as the mouth opened and a gurgling sound came out.

Tooth jumped up and immediately the boat began to rock.

"Sit down," cried Tank.

"You sit down. That thing is right here," shouted Tooth, jumping out of the boat on the shore side.

Tank couldn't retain his balance as Tooth leaped out. He fell backwards over the side of the boat hitting the water, just as an arm came up around his head.

"It's got me," screamed Tank, as he pushed back away from the awful thing in the water.

"I see it," said Wart. "There it is. It's right beside the boat. It's got Tank."

The General could no longer stand being on the shore. He leaped into the water and swam in the direction of the now overturned aluminum boat. As he swam, he kept growling through bared teeth. Whatever was in the water, he didn't like it.

Tank's head popped up on the shore side of the boat. "Where did it go?" he shouted.

Everyone was shouting and the General kept

barking as the group converged on the area around the small boat.

"Quiet," Moe shouted. "Everyone shut up."

Even the General stopped growling as the entire group looked around. Again the night became silent as eight pairs of eyes, including the General, scanned the surface of the river.

"Did you see it?" asked Moe.

"Only the eyes," answered Tank.

"I saw its face," said Tooth. "It was trying to talk. I swear. It was trying to talk to me."

Just then Beau gave out a loud scream. Something had tried to drag him under the water, or at least that's what it felt like.

"It's here. Help," he yelled. "It's got me."

The General again barked and growled ferociously. Dill dove into the water behind Beau as Wart and Moe surrounded him.

"*Ieeeeeooooowwww,*" shouted Dill as he came to the surface.

Moe grabbed hold of something that felt like an arm and pulled towards shore with all his might. Wart began smashing his fists back and forth at the object that floated behind Moe. Dill jumped on top of the dark form just as Wart let loose with a wild right roundhouse that caught Dill in the side of the head.

"Don't hit me," cried Dill. "Hit it."

Finally Beau, Tooth, Eep and the General all jumped on or tugged at the thing as Moe pulled it up on the riverbank.

"What is that?" asked Eep.

"I think it's a body, but it's been cut in half," said Tooth.

"It's not real," said Wart. "Look. The head is metal and its mouth just works up and down."

When Wart grabbed the mouth, the creature began to make noises.

"Follow me. I'll show you the way," it said.

"That's what Mrs. Wheatly said she heard," said

Eep.

"Yeah. That's right," said Wart. "It's a mechanical man that talks, but where did it come from?"

"The circus," said a deep voice from behind them. "There was a wreck above town on Thursday morning and they just pulled the truck out of Big Mountain Creek late this afternoon."

Chief of Police Elmer Todd stood on the riverbank a few feet from where the boys had dragged the mechanical man.

"You have been making so much noise down here that Mrs. Townes thought I should investigate. I thought I told you boys not to get involved."

"But, Chief, if we hadn't caught it tonight, it would have made it out into the channel and we would never have found out what was scaring everyone," said Moe.

"I guess you're right, but the next time you boys do something like this, I want to know what you're up to. *Kapisch*?"

All seven boys nodded their heads affirm-
atively.

"Yes, sir, but we were only trying to help," said
Moe.

"I know, son, but do you realize that if one of
you had gotten hurt, I would have to be the one to
tell your parents. Do you think that's fair to me or
to them?"

"No, sir. I didn't think about it that way."

"Well, you did good. You found out what was
happening in the river and you're all safe. That's
what counts. And I'm proud of you guys. You did
a good job of detective work. Just next time, let me
in on what you're doing."

"Yes, sir," said Moe. "We will."

"Do you think we can get that thing in the
boat?" asked Chief Todd.

"Sure, no problem," said Moe.

The boys brought Jim Hampton's yacht into

shore and turned it over to get the water out of it. It took all of them to lift the mechanical man into the boat, which they then pushed back into the water and began pulling up stream towards the ferryboat landing.

"I'll meet you there in a few minutes," said the Chief.

"This has sure been the best vacation I've ever had," said Beau.

Chapter Twenty-Five

❧—The River Rats along with Lucy, Alexis and Deanie walked down to the City Park, thinking that riding the midway rides would be fun. When the boys were mobbed with all kinds of people shaking their hands, hugging them and telling them that they were heroes, it felt good for a little while, but it quickly became embarrassing.

After about an hour of fame and excitement, the group decided that they would go home, planning to come back that night for the closing ceremonies and fireworks.

"Good evening, ladies and gentlemen," said Chet Snow, Mayor of Monley. The last few days have been a challenge for all of us, but these seven young men were equal to the task."

The Mayor asked all seven River Rats, including

Beau, to stand.

Looking out at the crowd, he said, "Please join me in congratulating these young men." With that, he began applauding.

The whole crowd soon began applauding and shouting. The River Rats' parents stood front and center, smiling and applauding along with the rest of the town.

Finally after several minutes of clapping and cheering, the mayor stepped back to the microphone.

"I think you all will agree that we have the best young people anywhere and these young men are an example of Monley's finest." After a slight pause, he continued, "If you seven will join me, we'll start the fireworks."

The River Rats, Beau and the Mayor pushed a large switch forward and immediately a rocket soared into the night sky, exploding with first a shower of red, then white and finally blue sparkles.

The crowd again erupted into cheers and applause as several more rockets lifted off. The crowd began to *ooh* and *aah* as the lights on the stage went out and more rockets burst against the darkened sky.

The River Rats left the stage and began to mingle through the crowd. Men patted them on the back, while ladies hugged them and said how brave they were.

Dill excused himself from two old ladies as he saw Deanie walking through the crowd. He hurried to catch up to her. He knew that she and her family would be leaving in the morning and he wanted to spend a last evening with her.

Patriotic music started blaring through the loud speakers.

When the last of the rockets had burst across the evening sky and the music had come to a close, the River Rats, along with the girls, headed towards home. They walked along their favorite part of town, the river. On their way, they saw the ferryboat loading up cars making their trip to Ohio.

"Anyone want to ride over to Ohio and back?" Eep asked.

"Nah, I'm ready to head home," said Wart.

"Me too," said Tooth.

"We've got to get up early in the morning," said Beau. "Dad says we're leaving at five-thirty."

"No, he didn't," said Alexis.

"Yeah, he did. He told Mom this afternoon. He said he wanted to get to St. Louis if possible by tomorrow night."

"Oh, great. I guess we sleep in the car again."

"Do you guys really have to leave so soon?" Dill asked Deanie.

"When Dad gets something set in his mind, that's it. I guess we'll be in St. Louis tomorrow night."

"Well, when are you coming back?"

"I don't know," she answered. "Hopefully next

summer."

Dill and Deanie walked a little slower than the others as they rounded the corner leading past the woods.

"Do you think there was ever anything   to what Al Dristen was talking about?" Tooth asked Wart. "You know, the Mountain Man?"

"Al is nuts. He's always been nuts. Does that answer your question?"

Dill and Deanie, now a half-block behind the others, stopped in the shadows. They looked at each other for a moment then Dill put his arm around her shoulder.

"I'm going to miss you," he said.

"Me too," she answered. "This has been the best, most exciting vacation we ever had. I hope we can come back and visit Aunt Ellie and Uncle Jim next summer."

Dill leaned closer and Deanie reached up and kissed him. The rest of the way home they held hands. Neither noticed the pair of red eyes that had been watching them from behind the trees. The underbrush was too thick to see much of anything in the daylight let alone in the dark. As the couple turned to head for home each thought they heard someone chuckling from back in the trees. They moved a little faster to catch up to the rest of the group.

Chapter Twenty-Six

❧Dill jumped up out of bed and threw on his clothes. He ran barefoot out the back door and leaped all three steps with a single bound, landing on the dewy grass. His alarm clock had gone off at exactly five-thirty, and it was still dark out. He hoped he would get to say goodbye to Deanie before her family left for Oklahoma.

Running down the alley, he rounded the corner of the Hamptons' garage just as the Smiths' station wagon pulled out of the driveway.

"Goodbye," he yelled.

Deanie leaned out of the rear window and hollered, "Write to me."

Pulling her head back in the window, she looked out the back window and waved. Just as they were about out of sight, Dill thought he saw Deanie blow him a kiss.

ABOUT THE AUTHOR

Hank Racer grew up in Sistersville, W. Va., along the banks of the Ohio River. With his cousins and friends, he swam in the muddy river and roamed the hills and valleys surrounding his hometown. It was during this time that he developed a love of reading and writing.

Today he lives in Florida with his wife Jan and their Chihuahua Morgan.